# ALPHA AND OMEGA™

## THE JUNIOR NOVEL

Adapted by Aaron Rosenberg
Original Script by Chris Denk

## SCHOLASTIC INC.

New York   Toronto   London   Auckland
Sydney   Mexico City   New Delhi   Hong Kong

ISBN 978-0-545-21461-2

12 11 10 9 8 7 6 5 4 3 2 1          10 11 12 13 14 15/0

Designed by Rick DeMonico
Printed in the U.S.A.                                          40
First printing, September 2010

Dear Reader,

I hope you enjoyed watching Kate and Humphrey in *Alpha and Omega*. I had a blast working on the movie! My castmates were fantastic, and it was really cool to see them animate my character, Kate, around my voice. However, what really drew me into the story of *Alpha and Omega* was the focus on wolves and the environment.

Wolves in real life are a bit different than the ones in the movie. In many areas, wolves are virtually extinct and their lives in the wild are even more complicated. Fewer natural wildlife habitat areas are left each year for wolves and other animals. Even worse, the habitats that remain are often downgraded to have little similarity to the natural wildlife areas that have existed in the past, and that prevents animals from finding food and safe places to live.

These animals are significantly important to maintaining the natural balance in our ecosystems, and they are endangered species which we risk losing if we don't preserve adequate amounts of habitat for their survival. Helping make our planet a cleaner, greener place for all of us to live is very important to me—especially when it comes to saving animals. Scientists are working extremely hard to help get the wolf population up—but it's a tough job!

Wolves need the help of people like you and me, and I think we could all work together to help support the repopulation and protection of these animals. There are many ways to get involved—like recycling, conserving energy, and keeping our communities clean. But if you want to do more, you can get informed by reading books, taking classes, or even volunteering at wildlife organizations. With understanding we can all make a difference in the lives of these beautiful creatures.

So get out there and go green. You will help wolves like Kate and Humphrey live a little longer!

Your friend,

Hayden

# PROLOGUE

I t was fall in Canada's Jasper Park, a beautiful nature reserve. Animals roamed freely: hunting, grazing, and running through the tall grass, beneath the tall trees, and along the gleaming lakes.

Four young wolves were currently at the top of the hill pushing a log into position.

"Guys, guys, guys!" their leader, Humphrey, shouted, encouraging them on to greater efforts. "It's time to ride the slide and taste the wind!"

His best friend, Salty, wagged his head. "Humphrey, you are totally genius!" Salty was the laid-back, cheerful member of the quartet.

Humphrey grinned at him in return, tongue

lolling from the side of his mouth. "Come on, guys!" he urged. "Let's go!"

They gave one final push and the log rolled into place. Then Mooch, whose bulk was as much fat as muscle, shoved the front end and the log swiveled around, angling straight back down the hill. It teetered for a second, before slipping downward in the mud. All four wolves leaped onto it. Humphrey was in front, of course, with Mooch in back, and Salty and clever little Shakey in between.

All at once something beneath them scraped and snapped, and suddenly the log tilted forward and plummeted down the hill!

"Air wolf!" Humphrey shouted as they careened downward. The wind whipped at his face and tugged at his fur as they raced down the hill. He couldn't believe he'd never thought of this before! This was amazing!

Nearby, another young wolf was playing in her own way.

Kate leaped out of the bushes and landed in front

of a smaller wolf. She put her head down, tail up and wagging, front legs bent, back legs stiff. Classic pouncing posture.

"This caribou is mine!" she growled.

"Kate!" her intended prey whined, backing away and almost tripping over her own tail. "I'm not a caribou, I'm your sister!"

Kate ignored Lilly's pleas. In her mind's eye she didn't see her younger sister; she saw a lone caribou, trembling with fear. She tensed, then leaped. The "caribou" bleated in alarm and bolted, but Kate had expected that and her jump carried her right into its path.

"You can't escape the greatest Alpha ever!" she bragged. And she would be! The Alphas were the leaders, the hunters, and she was destined to be one, just like her father, Winston, who ruled the western pack, and her mother, Eve. She'd make them proud.

She was so busy taunting her prey, however, that she didn't see the tree right in front of her.

*Wham!* Kate ran headfirst into its trunk. The impact knocked her back on her haunches.

"Some great Alpha!" Lilly teased as she kept running.

"Oh, yeah?" Kate shook her head again to clear it, then staggered back to her feet. "Just for that, you're lunch!" She bolted after her sister, focused on catching Lilly and pinning her before she could make it back to the family den.

Meanwhile, the boys were starting to get a bit worried. The ride had been fun at first, even for the more timid Mooch and Shakey, but it had already gone on a bit too long—and it showed no sign of slowing.

"Oh!" Mooch moaned as they narrowly missed a tree. "We're all gonna die!"

Even Humphrey was starting to get worried. "What was I thinking?" he wondered out loud, but he knew the answer already. He hadn't been. He was an Omega wolf, supposed to keep the peace, maintain calm, and help smooth over relations with other wolves—yet here he was, goofing off and having fun. And now he and his friends were in danger!

Humphrey spotted several rocks up ahead, and

felt a chill. If they hit those at this speed, the log would get shattered to kindling—and them with it! He had to do something! But what?

Then he had it! "Roll left!" he shouted to his pals. Obediently, they all shuffled their paws to the left—and the log rolled with them! Yes!

They swept safely past the rocks. But Humphrey hadn't noticed a fallen log forming a ramp in their new path, and they hit that and shot off it and into the air!

Humphrey was thrilled. He hadn't even considered the possibility of flying! "That was great!" he shouted over his shoulder as the log landed, the impact sending a shudder through him but not dislodging him from his perch. "We are flying today, guys!"

The others didn't answer—probably enjoying the ride too much to speak, Humphrey decided. He saw a boulder straight ahead of them, its surface also angled upward, and crouched down. The log hit the boulder and went airborne again, but this time Humphrey didn't manage to stay on. The log dropped back down but he flew higher, nothing but air riffling his fur all around. "Woo-hoo!"

There! Kate saw something shift in a bush just ahead of her. Lilly was hiding there—she knew it! Without slowing down, Kate pushed down with her hind legs to launch herself into the air. She shot forward, bounding over the bush so she could pounce on Lilly from behind—

—and yelped when she sailed past. The bush had been at the top of a small outcropping, and now she was leaping into thin air! There was nothing else up here, and the ground was awfully far below!

"Kate?" she heard her sister call out from safely under the bush, but Kate was no longer thinking about her, or about the hunt. She was just wondering what would happen when she eventually came down!

Humphrey saw something in the air in front of him, and whipped his head around. Whatever it was, it was brown and approaching fast.

*　*　*

Something appeared in Kate's field of vision and she squinted. What was that? It was gray and right in front of her — and closing in fast.

The two wolves recognized each other at the same time.

"Kate?" Humphrey called out.

"Humphrey?" she replied.

Then they slammed into each other — face-first! They reached out, latching onto each other's paws, and the force of their impact spun them both around so they circled in midair.

It was a magical moment. They had grown up together, of course, and had always gotten along well, though Kate was an Alpha while Humphrey was an Omega. But now they couldn't help but be aware of each other.

Then their own momentum pulled them apart again.

"What are you doing up here?" Humphrey asked,

finding his voice first though it caught a bit. He was still reeling from their collision. . . .

"I'm practicing hunting for our lunch," Kate told him proudly.

"Oh, good," he replied, grinning. "'Cause I'm about to lose mine."

"You are? *Eww!*" Kate recoiled.

"I'll try to swallow it," he assured her, and she realized he'd been kidding. As usual. Humphrey was never serious about anything.

Suddenly the ground interrupted her musing and drove all thought from her head and all breath from her lungs.

*Wham!*

"*Uhh!*" Humphrey moaned as he crashed down, too. They rolled to a stop right next to each other, and for a second they gazed into each other's eyes, both a bit stunned.

Kate was back on her feet first, as usual. "You okay?" she asked him, shaking off her own aches and pains.

"Sure, fine, never better," he claimed, though it took him two tries to regain his paws. "You?"

"No worries." She started to say more, though she had no idea what, when someone called her name.

"Kate!" A massive wolf just edging past his prime stood near the edge of the woods, his deep voice echoing out through the trees. It was her father, Winston!

"It's time to go," he told her. She nodded and shook off the last of the impact.

"I'm coming, Dad!" she assured him, and scampered over to join him, excitement making her fur tingle. She'd forgotten what day it was!

"Where are you going?" Humphrey asked, following her.

Her dad heard his question. "She's going to Alpha school, Humphrey," he explained, pride clear in the rumble of his voice. "My little girl is going to learn how to be a strong Alpha wolf!" He nudged Kate with the tip of his nose, and she pranced happily, her tail wagging fiercely.

"I will, I will!" she promised. She'd been looking forward to this since her parents had first realized she was an Alpha—when Lilly had been a newborn and she'd pinned her to the ground.

"Kate will marry another Alpha one day," Winston was saying, "and they will be the new leaders of the pack." That was a long way in the future, though, and Kate didn't think about any of that. All she knew was that she was going to get trained to be a real Alpha! Sure, she'd miss her parents and Lilly and her friends, but it was only for one season! "She'll be back in the spring," Winston said, echoing her thoughts.

"Spring?" Humphrey didn't look any happier. "But that's a whole winter away!"

"That'll give you plenty of time to work on your Omega skills before you meet again, Humphrey," Winston reminded him gently but firmly. "I need the Alphas to hunt and lead, but I need the Omegas to keep the peace and keep the pack nice and—"

He was interrupted as three young wolves suddenly leaped out and tackled Humphrey.

"Wolf pile!" Salty, Mooch, and Shakey shouted as they piled onto their friend. The four of them collapsed into a heap in the mud at Winston and Kate's feet.

"—calm," Winston finished, shaking his head. He couldn't completely hide his smile, however. Though an Alpha himself, he was wise enough to recognize the value of both Alphas and Omegas, and affectionate enough to still be amused by the antics and good natures of these young pack members.

"Come on, Kate, let's go," he reminded her gently, brushing his shoulder against hers.

"Right, okay. Bye, Humphrey," she said, but Humphrey was too busy wrestling to notice.

"Don't worry, sir," he called out. "Omega class is already in session!" But when Winston didn't reply, Humphrey squirmed around to where he could see past his friends. He watched as Winston and Kate walked away. "Good-bye, Kate," he whispered. Then Mooch bit his ear, and Humphrey turned his attention back to the mock battle. Somewhere beneath his playful growls, however, there was a sad whimper at the thought that his friend had gone, and a grim whisper that the next time he saw her they would both be very different.

# CHAPTER ONE

L et's ride, boys!"

Humphrey leaped onto the log. Over the winter he'd gained his full height and started to fill out. He was a handsome young wolf, and there was an air of confidence and casualness about him that put others at ease. When he wasn't up to something crazy—like logboarding.

"Wahoo!" Salty shouted. He jumped onto the log after Humphrey. Shakey and Mooch were right behind him. The four of them had spent countless hours practicing their logboarding throughout the cold winter months. They were experts now.

The log sped down the hill and over a short cliff. None of them fell off, however. Instead all four wolves twisted to the left at the same time, their claws still planted firmly in the log's bark and wood. Their movement shifted the log beneath them, and it swiveled to the side, turning all the way around before it came down on the ground in a clear patch between trees. It didn't lose any speed.

The trees were coming up fast, but Humphrey didn't panic. "Angle left, thirty degrees!" he ordered. They shuffled their feet to the left a step, and the log obligingly shifted with them. It slid between the tree trunks, close enough that a few small branches ruffled Humphrey's fur.

Now they were starting to slow a bit, as the rocky ground tore up their momentum. They needed a boost. "Salty!" Humphrey told his best friend. "Give us some sail draft."

Salty stood on his hind legs, front paws outspread. He angled slightly to the side, until his body was directly in the wind—it shoved against him, pushing him faster and the log with him. He was a living sail!

Salty had his eyes closed and his head back,

tongue lolling out. "I think I taste the wind," he whispered. Then he coughed, hacked, and spit something out of his mouth. "No, just a bug." The others laughed.

Humphrey was keeping a steady eye on their progress, though. "Hey, Mooch, get ready," he warned. Mooch gave him a paws-up. Humphrey waited, gauging the distance as they approached a boulder still covered in snow and ice. It formed a perfect ramp. "Lower the boom!" he shouted finally.

Mooch sank down on his rear at the back of the log. Always chunky, he had become downright plump during the winter despite the lack of available food, and now his heavy backside drove the log's end into the ground—and angled the front up into the air. They hit the ramp perfectly, sliding along and up it, and then shot off into the air.

They all cheered and howled. They loved the thrill of racing down the mountainside like this. What had they done before logboarding?

Humphrey knew, though, that their skills weren't complete. "Guys," he pointed out, "we really need to work on the—" His eyes widened as he saw a huge boulder suddenly emerge from the snow-covered bushes. It was right in front of them!

"—brakes!" he finished, bracing for impact.

"Brakes?" the others echoed. Then Shakey and Mooch gasped as they saw the boulder, too.

It was too late to do anything. With a loud crash the log smashed into the boulder full-force. Its front end splintered, flipping the log up and over, and all four wolves went flying.

"*Aaaah!*" Humphrey landed first. He let out a second "*Oof!*" as Salty and then Shakey dropped on top of him. Then a shadow loomed overhead, cutting off the sun, and he glanced up. "Oh, no!" It was Mooch!

"Wolf pile!" Mooch shouted as he plummeted toward them. He squashed the three of them flat, his enormous rear firmly in Shakey's face. Shakey complained good-naturedly, and they all laughed and rolled on the ground. Another logboarding run successfully completed!

Salty had a question, though. "What did we hit?" He hadn't noticed the boulder.

Humphrey glanced around, and realized that he wasn't lying in snow. There was nothing but grass beneath him. And off to the side he saw flowers peeking up around the boulders and trees. Overhead, a few birds began to chirp.

"Spring!" he answered. He grinned, and his buddies grinned back at him. They had enjoyed their games in the snow, but food was always scarce during the winter. Now, with spring returning, the caribou and other prey would be back as well. Warm weather, good food—they had plenty to look forward to.

Then Humphrey caught a flicker of movement down in the valley below. He twisted around, pulling himself free from the wolf pile, and crept closer for a better look. What was it?

He grinned when he was able to see more clearly. There was a young female wolf stalking through the grass down there. She was tall and strong and lovely, her brown fur gleaming in the sun, and Humphrey recognized her immediately. "Whoa," he whispered. "Look who's back from Alpha school." It was Kate!

She wasn't alone, either. There were six other wolves with her. Humphrey knew them all—they were Alphas for the western pack, his pack. Kate was in the lead, and from here he could see her target. Two caribou stood alone in the middle of the valley, grazing on the first of the fresh spring grass, unaware of the hungry wolves creeping toward them.

The others had come up beside Humphrey and had noticed the focus of his attention. "Forget about it, Humphrey," Salty warned. "Kate's an Alpha now. And you're an Omega."

Humphrey knew what his friend was saying. Alphas and Omegas didn't mix. Oh, they could talk, share food, but they couldn't mate. It wasn't allowed. He swallowed and put on a casual tone. "We're friends, okay?"

"Exactly," Mooch agreed. "Just friends." Humphrey sighed. His friends knew him too well to be fooled that easily.

"You better set your sights over there, instead," Salty advised. He gestured off to the side, where a pair of young female wolves had emerged from some bushes. Squirrels scurried along the branches, and at first Humphrey thought they were leaping into the girls' mouths. Talk about an easy meal! But then he realized they were shoving something else at the wolves instead. Berries. They were feeding the girls berries!

"Hey, Reba! Hey, Janice!" Salty called out. The girls turned and smiled at them. Their lips were stained red from berry juice.

"Be nice to your furry friends," Reba encouraged them.

"Don't eat them!" Janice agreed.

The squirrels tossed more berries into the girls' mouths. That was just weird!

Humphrey shook his head. "O-kay." But he leaned against Salty and muttered, "I'll stick to meat, thanks—and to girls that like it, too."

"Seriously," Salty agreed. They turned their backs on Reba and Janice and paced toward the side of the cliff, where they could watch the hunt that was still unfolding below.

*    *    *

Kate was totally focused. She and her team crept through the grass without a sound, each paw precisely placed. The caribou continued to graze, unaware. When she judged they were close enough, Kate nudged her second, Can-Do. He in turn nudged Hutch. The three of them split off to the left, while the other three continued on around to the east. They'd circle the caribou and then, when they were on either side, pounce. Trapped between them, the caribou wouldn't have a chance.

Kate resisted the urge to howl with delight. Here she was, just back from Alpha school, and already leading her first hunt! She loved the thrill of closing on the prey and the pride at the thought that tonight she would be providing much-needed food for her pack. This is what life was all about!

Watching from up above, Humphrey was impressed. Kate looked so calm, so confident, so completely in control! "Looks like we're eating caribou tonight, boys," he whispered to his friends.

But then Mooch started. "Hey, hey." He pointed past the hunting scene, to the far side of the valley. Two large wolves were sneaking across the valley floor!

Humphrey's eyes narrowed and his teeth bared as he recognized them: Scar and Claw. "Eastern pack wolves," he muttered. This could be trouble!

Kate didn't notice the intrusion. She was too busy concentrating on the hunt. "*Psst!*" she whispered to her teammates. "Can-Do. Hutch. We're going in!"

They both nodded, and the three of them stalked forward together. The other team was on the far side. Kate could just make out their eyes through the grass. Everyone was in position. A few paces closer, and—

*Woof! Woof! Woof!*

She jumped as barking and growling cut through the quiet. What? Nobody on her team would be that stupid! Rising from her crouch she glanced around, just in time to see Scar and Claw appear and launch themselves at the caribou. *Agh!*

But the two eastern pack wolves had misjudged the distance. They were too far away to pounce, and the pair of caribou snorted in alarm and wheeled to run — straight toward Kate!

She faltered to the side, just evading a strike from the lead caribou's heavy hooves, and then spun and dove for its hind legs, head outstretched, jaws open to bite —

— and fell to the ground, wincing, as her teeth closed on a few strands of fur and nothing more. Missed!

The caribou were running now, with Scar and Claw right behind them. Kate was furious. Those eastern pack wolves had spoiled her hunt! If Scar and Claw thought they were going to claim the prey as well, they had another thought coming! She went after them, teeth bared. Her teammates were right behind her.

Kate charged down the valley, losing sight of first the caribou and then the intruding wolves as they disappeared around a bend. A second later the two eastern pack wolves reappeared again . . . but this time they were heading back toward Kate! And as they approached she saw that their eyes were wide with fear. What had spooked them like that? She got her answer as a rumble rose from somewhere ahead of her, loud enough to make her head throb and deep enough to shake the earth beneath her paws. Something was coming! Something big!

Kate gasped as the rumbling increased and a mass of roiling brown and gray and black appeared around the bend. It was a stampede!

Turning on her heels, she raced back the way she had come. "Scatter!" she called out to her team. "To the sides!" They reacted instantly, running full tilt toward the valley's sloping sides. The caribou wouldn't follow them up there—when they were stampeding all the beasts wanted was a clear path, and that meant going straight down the valley, from one end to the other.

Right over Kate.

She dodged a flying hoof, ducked beneath a leaping caribou stag, tumbled to avoid being trampled by a pair of bulls, and twisted to keep her paws from being smashed by a medium-sized doe. Each twist and turn brought Kate closer to the side, and finally she gathered herself into a crouch, coiled, and took off, stretching forward as she leaped. There was a small hill along the valley's side, and Kate landed neatly there, taking only one step before willing her legs to stop and turning to watch the rest of the stampede gallop past. Safe!

But, she realized an instant later, not everyone had been so lucky.

All of her hunting party had gotten safely out of the way, but there were two wolves still down there: Scar and Claw. They were running for their lives, and they were out in front of the caribou . . . for now. But they wouldn't be able to maintain that pace for long. For an instant Kate considered turning her back—after all, they were trespassing. But if she did they'd be trampled for sure, and she couldn't let that happen. "Settle the score later," she reminded herself. An Alpha didn't leave another wolf behind.

Taking a deep breath, Kate bounded down from

the hill. She was behind the herd now, and she put on a spurt of speed, flying past them along the side. Soon she was catching up with the leading caribous—and with Scar and Claw.

A small embankment presented itself, and Kate raced along it. When she neared its edge she didn't hesitate. Instead she hurled herself forward, right off the embankment and down into the valley.

She had judged the distance perfectly.

*Wham!* She landed atop Scar and Claw, knocking both eastern pack wolves from their feet. All three of them rolled to the side—and right behind a small hill there. The caribou poured on past, oblivious. Safe again!

As the dust cleared and the rumbling faded into the distance, Kate's teammates approached. "Are you all right?" Hutch asked her.

"Yeah, I'm fine," she assured him, hopping to her feet. And she was. Physically.

Can-Do, on the other hand, had ignored her and gone straight for Claw. "Hey, what's your problem?" Can-Do demanded. "You stupid eastern dog!

That was our hunt! You can't just snake it out from under us!"

Kate padded over to them. "Can-Do," she said, "back off!"

Claw didn't help matters any by grinning down at Can-Do, who was half his size. "You better listen to the girl," Claw warned. Beside him, Scar grinned and snapped his massive jaws.

Can-Do wasn't that easily intimidated, though. He started snarling at the eastern pack wolves, daring them to try anything. Hutch and the others joined in. But Scar and Claw didn't show any signs of backing down.

"Hey, break it up!" she insisted, but this time her teammates ignored her. Any second now they were going to go for one another's throats.

Just then a voice from somewhere nearby called out, "Stampede!"

Everyone froze. After a second they all started glancing around. Kate didn't hear any rumbling, though.

She did, however, see a lean gray shape slide

down into the valley and approach them. Another wolf, around her age by the look of him, and an Omega considering the easy way he carried himself. Something about him seemed really familiar, too.

He apparently knew her already. "Kate," he greeted her once he was by her side.

The voice was what clued her in. "Humphrey?" She was amazed. Her old playmate had grown up!

Can-Do was still growling. "I'm gonna tear these snaggletoothed fools apart," he claimed, snarling at Scar.

But Humphrey slid in between them. "Guys, guys," he said, "come on. Don't get your fur in a bunch." His tone was friendly, casual, and it helped put the others at ease as he continued. "You guys are making us look bad. Come on, the caribou are laughing at us." He gestured to the far end of the valley, where a large group of caribou had lined up. As they watched, the caribou all turned their backs on the wolves and swayed their butts, deliberately taunting them.

Humphrey sighed and shook his head. "Now

there's a moon I don't want to howl to," he muttered. Can-Do heard him and actually laughed. So did Scar. The rest laughed as well. Even Kate chuckled. Humphrey was really good at this!

"Now, what do you say, guys?" he asked playfully, stepping up in front of Scar and Claw. "Why don't you go hunt on the east side where you belong, hmm?" From Can-Do or one of the other Alphas that remark would have been a challenge, but Humphrey's tone was so light it was like he was buddies with them and just teasing them a bit. How could they take offense?

Before Scar or Claw could respond, a voice yelled, "Western hunt group!"

They all turned to see Kate's father poised at the top of a nearby hill. The winter had turned his muzzle gray, but he was still a powerful Alpha and a strong leader. "Get back to the den," he commanded, and Kate's team hastened to obey. "The two of you," he continued, glaring at Scar and Claw, "go home." They started to snarl, and Winston bared his fangs. "Now!" The thunder in his voice cowed them, and the two turned tail and fled, trying to look as if they weren't scared.

Winston waited as Humphrey and Kate loped up to join him. "Humphrey," Winston started. His tone softened. "Good job."

Humphrey grinned, pleased with himself. He'd impressed the pack leader!

Kate was less enthused. "My first hunt and I blew it," she complained, her voice edging toward a whine.

"Aw, don't beat yourself up," Humphrey told her. "You were amazing. Besides, if anyone is hungry they can eat . . ." He trailed off, thinking furiously. Then something chattered in his ear. He glanced over. Two of Reba and Janice's tame squirrels were perched on a branch beside him. They held up smaller branches covered in dark red berries.

". . . berries," Humphrey finished. "They can eat berries!"

He popped a pawful of berries into his mouth and chewed, juice spraying everywhere. Ugh! These things were gross! But he couldn't stand to see Kate so upset. "They're really, um, nutritious," he managed, still chewing.

"Yeah, tell that to a hungry pack," Kate muttered. She stalked off, tail down, and Humphrey spit out the rest of the berries—all over the squirrels.

"Sorry, guys," he told them absently as he followed Kate back to the den. He hoped he'd be able to find some other way to cheer Kate up.

# CHAPTER TWO

**K**ate trailed Winston back to the large hillside that served as the western pack's home. Caves all along the hillside had been turned into dens, and each had a small plateau in front of it. As the pack leader, Winston and his family held the top plateau. Eve, Winston's mate and Kate and Lilly's mother, was waiting for them when they returned. Lilly was with her.

Eve glanced up as Winston and Kate entered the den, a question clear in her eyes, but Winston spoke before she could ask. "Those eastern wolves ruined our hunt," he rasped. The anger that flared in Eve's eyes matched his own. Kate felt even worse. She knew they'd been counting on her and her hunting party to bring back food for everyone.

Lilly tried cheering Kate up by dangling her tail over her head, but Kate wasn't in the mood to laugh. "Kate, you're slouching," Eve scolded her at dinner, but gently. That was typical of her: sweet but strong. "There, that's better. Thank you, honey. See how strong and beautiful you are?" But all Kate could see was her failure. They had nothing to eat but scraps, and they were the pack leader's family! She could only imagine how much worse the rest of the pack had it.

Winston seemed to feel the same way. "Scraps and bones is no kind of dinner," he growled. "Not for my pack!"

"I'm sorry, Dad," Kate told him. "It's just those eastern wolves—"

He cut her off. "It's not your fault, Kate," he insisted. "Those two are entirely to blame. What they did was wrong in many ways. When they crossed into our territory they broke pack law."

"What are you going to do, Dad?" Lilly asked. But before he could reply someone called to him from outside. It was Hutch, Winston's second in command, who had accompanied Kate on her hunt earlier. Winston rose to speak with him, and Kate followed quietly.

"Are we just going to let them keep raiding our hunts?" Hutch was saying when she crept close enough to listen.

"Of course not," her father answered. "Put our Alphas on alert."

"Already done, sir," Hutch told him. Glancing around, Kate saw that he was right. All along the edge of the valley she saw Alphas standing ready for trouble. She also saw Humphrey talking to several other wolves.

Turning away from watching Humphrey, Kate realized Winston had vanished. Where had he gone? She scoured the valley and after a minute she made out a dark shadow moving quickly toward the far end of the valley. What was he doing? Well, whatever it was, she intended to be by his side. Setting her ears back, Kate took off after her father.

Kate watched from behind a clump of bushes as Winston stood on a tall cliff and howled. After a second, a distant howl answered him. With a flick of his tail Winston left the cliff and continued on his way. Kate waited until he had almost passed out of sight before sneaking after him.

Winston finally slowed in a small clearing. Kate had never seen this place before, and she wasn't sure she liked it—mist curled through the trees and across the ground, hiding any prints and making it look as if she were walking through a cloud. It was eerily quiet, and she shivered from both the cold breeze and the damp chill that clung to the place. Why would her father come here?

She got her answer a minute later when another wolf emerged from the mist and stalked toward him. Slinking back behind a tree, Kate repressed a gasp. It was Tony! The head of the eastern pack was even bigger than her father, though his fur was also more grizzled with silver and white. His gait was slightly stiff, but there was still power in his limbs and his fangs still looked sharp.

"Winston," he growled as he approached her father.

"Tony," Winston replied. He didn't seem the least bit frightened of the other wolf. If anything, he seemed almost friendly as he added, "You're looking good."

The mist parted enough to reveal a small creek running through the clearing, and Tony jumped over it. He landed awkwardly, however, and grimaced. "Oh, whoa," he whined, "my back feels like wood. I got this disc that keeps cracking. It drives me crazy!"

"Yeah, Tony," Winston agreed dryly, "you're one crazy wolf."

"Yeah?" Tony scowled and paced sideways, circling around Winston. Winston shifted to keep facing him.

"Yeah. Like that little game of tag your boys played during our hunt," Winston told his fellow leader. "Let's leave the games to the Omegas, hmm?"

"You know there's no caribou left in the east," Tony growled.

"You've got a problem, then." Winston's tone, and the rumble behind his words, made it clear he felt Tony should keep his problems to himself and his pack.

Tony's tone suddenly changed. "Unite the packs, Winston," he wheedled. "That's what you promised, isn't it? It was you who gave me that big speech that your daughter Kate, and my son, Garth, would marry and bring us all together."

Kate was stunned. Her father had promised her to Tony's son?

"Garth knows his responsibility," Tony continued. "Does Kate?"

"Don't worry," Winston replied. "She knows."

*I do?* Kate thought. But in a way, she did. She'd always known she would serve her pack as best she could. And if that meant marrying this Garth fellow? So be it.

"Good," Tony said. "Then she can meet Garth tonight at the moonlight howl."

"Fine." Winston turned to go.

But Tony wasn't finished. "This had better work, Winston," he warned. "If we have to, we'll fight for the valley."

Winston turned and fixed Tony with his steely glare, the one that made even the biggest Alpha cower like a cub. "That would be a big mistake," he stated. Tony shrugged off the look and disappeared back into the mist. The mist was clearing slightly, and as Winston took a step toward home it parted enough for Kate to see him clearly—and for him to see her as well.

"Kate?" He looked surprised, confused, and a little embarrassed. "I, uh—"

"It's okay, Dad," she assured him. "I understand. It's my responsibility."

Her father sighed. "I'm sorry," he told her softly, nuzzling her shoulder with his nose. "I never meant for you to find out this way."

"It's okay," she told him again. "Really." She nudged him back. "We should be getting home."

He nodded. "Your mother will be worried."

Kate laughed. "That and I've got a howl to prepare for."

As they left the clearing she wondered about her own reaction. A part of her was terrified and shocked—but a part of her was excited as well. Here was something she could do to help her pack! Something she could do to make her father proud! How could she say no?

# CHAPTER THREE

uys!" Humphrey caught up to his friends as they were playing some sort of game that involved directing squirrels to smack berries at each other across the den floor. "We gotta get ready for the moonlight howl. What are you doing?"

He got three blank stares in return. "The howl?" Salty asked.

Humphrey sighed. "You know," he reminded them. "Girls?"

That got their attention. This was the first howl they could participate in, after all, which meant it was their first chance to find mates. "Woohoo!" Salty howled. Shakey and Mooch joined in. Humphrey sighed again and shook his head. He loved them dearly, but they were seriously clueless.

Meanwhile, up in the leader's den, Lilly was helping her sister get ready.

"So," she asked as she teased Kate's fur with a pinecone brush, "are you nervous about marrying Garth?" Lilly stumbled over the words a bit, but that wasn't unusual. She'd always been the shy one of the two of them, even as a cub.

"Not really," Kate told her, trying to convince herself. "Besides, I have to. It's my responsibility, for our pack and for our home."

"Well, I hear he's really hot," Lilly whispered, her tail twirling with excitement. Her eyes shone from behind the hair that always fell in front of them.

Kate laughed. "Well, maybe you should marry him, then," she teased. Bad idea—Lilly started gasping for air and fell to the ground, terrified. "Calm down," Kate told her, rubbing her head gently. "I'm just kidding. You're an Omega and he's an Alpha. You know that's forbidden."

Lilly nodded, shuddered, and took a deep breath.

"Right, I knew that," she admitted, and scrambled back up. "Now let's finish getting you ready!"

"Oh, Kate," Eve said when the two girls finally emerged. "You look so beautiful." Her voice turned serious. "Now, if Garth gets out of line," she warned, "Take those beautiful teeth of yours, go for the throat, and don't let go until the body stops shaking."

Kate stared at her and Lilly gasped. Sometimes their mom frightened them!

"If you don't want to do this," Winston said slowly, "if you're not ready—"

"Don't worry, Dad," Kate assured him. "I'm ready." But deep down, she wondered if she really was.

"You guys look great," Humphrey told his buddies, trying not to laugh. His friends had been trying to groom themselves, but it hadn't exactly worked out. They looked ridiculous! "Tell you what—let me go ahead and prepare the girls for your arrival. You guys meet me there. We don't want them to be, you know, surprised by how awesome you look."

"Totally!" Salty agreed. He and Shakey and Mooch started slapping each other on the back. Humphrey slipped out while they were congratulating each other. Whew!

He loped over to Jasper Park's big central hill. The crescent moon was rising, and the hill was dotted with wolves, all broken into pairs. Single wolves lolled around the edges, seeking partners.

In the center, one pair of wolves was sniffing each other. After a minute the girl began to howl, her voice rising into the night. The boy joined in, and their voices blended together perfectly. A second pair followed suit, and then a third, and a fourth. Each pair sounded completely different, but each couple harmonized beautifully. That was how wolves knew they'd found their true mates, when their howls matched.

He heard a commotion behind him—someone shouting "Hey! Hey!"—and turned around. Salty, Shakey, and Mooch had almost caught up to him but had been distracted by a pair of young female wolves. Judging by his expression, Salty had tried to approach them and based upon their laughter, the ladies had shot him down. Typical.

"I saw the whole thing, guys," Humphrey told his buddies as he joined them, "and I can't believe they didn't fall all over you. And when you yelled 'Hey'—I mean, I thought you clinched it right there."

"Har-de-har-har," Salty replied, annoyed. "What, you think you can do better?"

"Oh, please." Humphrey puffed out his chest. "The next girl that come over the hill, she's mine."

Even as the words left his mouth he saw a young wolf appear at the base of the hill. It was Kate! And she looked amazing!

"I'll be right back," he told the others absently, starting toward her. But they jumped in his way.

"Where do you think you're going?" Mooch asked him.

"Come on, Humphrey, you know the rules," Salty added. "You're not allowed to howl with her. She's an Alpha." Shakey and Mooch nodded.

Humphrey sighed. "Yeah, I know, guys. But why is that? Just because some wolves a long time ago decided that they're up there and we're down here?"

"Cheer up, buddy," Salty suggested, slamming a shoulder against him. "You still got us."

"Yeah," Shakey agreed. "Friends for life!"

"Omegas!" Mooch hollered. The three of them jumped on Humphrey and began wrestling him until he couldn't help but laugh and join in. They all went down in a tangle and rolled right down the hill. Unfortunately, their path took them to the edge of a cliff. Salty, Shakey, and Mooch got hung up on the rocks along the edge, but Humphrey had wound up on top of the pile as they reached that edge, and when his friends jerked to a halt he sailed on, flying out over the cliff—

—and right into a tree.

*Oof!* He scrabbled for purchase on a branch and hung there, unable to climb up, but too high up to comfortably jump down. Great.

Things got even worse when he heard paws below. Glancing down, Humphrey saw two young female wolves stop right below the tree. Lilly . . . and Kate. Swell.

"So," Lilly was saying, "do you see Garth?"

"I'm not even sure what he looks like," Kate admitted. "But I'm sure—" Her voice trailed off, and Humphrey craned his neck to glance where she was looking. Through the leaves he could make out the top of the hill . . . and the tall, powerful-looking wolf standing there, silhouetted by the moon. There was no question that he was an Alpha, maybe even *the* Alpha.

"—we'll know him when we see him," Kate finished.

"Hey, hey, hey!" The handsome male wolf called down to them. "Kate!" He leaped down the hill, heading straight toward her, a perfect picture of grace and power.

"Yep," Humphrey muttered. "He's up there"—he could feel his grip slipping—"and I'm down here." Then he fell.

*Whump!*

He landed right between Kate, Lilly, and the new-comer, who could only be the eastern pack leader's son, Garth. The impact raised a cloud of dust that billowed up into Garth's face, sending him into a coughing fit.

"*Ow!* Oh, my butt, my butt," Humphrey whined, hopping to his feet and dancing around. "Wow, that really hurt. Hey, sorry to drop in on you." He winked at Garth. "You should really do something about that cough." Then he glanced at Kate. "Be careful, Kate," he warned playfully. "There's something going around. Tails and ears are falling right off. Literally." He waggled his before facing Garth again. "Name's Humphrey."

"Garth," the big newcomer growled.

"Wow, you are a big one, aren't you?" Humphrey asked, circling. "You're practically a moose! Where you hiding them antlers?"

Garth was clearly not amused. "Who's the coyote?" he asked Kate pointedly.

Humphrey bristled but tried to conceal it. Coyotes were like wolves' little cousins, smaller and weaker in every way. It was an insult, but he couldn't let it get to him. "Oh, I get it," he said instead. "No, that's good. Because I'm, like —"

"No one important," Kate interrupted sharply, giving him a glare. "Lilly, why don't you take little coyote Humphrey and run along?"

Lilly was staring at Garth, and Kate had to clear her throat loudly to get her attention, but finally Lilly started. "Oh, ah, right," she mumbled. "Come on, Humphrey."

"Who's he calling 'coyote'?" Humphrey grumbled under his breath as he let her drag him away. "Oh, I'll show you coyote." But he wasn't fooling anyone. There wasn't a thing he could do to Garth. Besides, Kate was an Alpha—it wasn't like he'd ever had a chance with her anyway.

Kate sighed. She felt bad about snapping at Humphrey, but she was trying to steel herself for the whole marriage thing, and his joking and teasing weren't helping any. Instead she took a deep breath and turned to face Garth. He was certainly handsome, anyway.

"So tell me about yourself," she suggested softly. "What do you like to do?"

"Oh, well," he frowned, clearly not used to being asked questions like that. "I'm, ah, really into fitness. You know, rabbit sprints, tree squats." He showed off several impressive exercise routines. "You know us Alphas, gotta keep fit to lead the pack." He winked at her. "But what really gets me going is" — he started to howl — "*Aaa-oooowwww!*"

It was all Kate could do not to bury her head between her paws. She'd never heard such a dreadful noise. He was awful!

All around them, other wolves stopped howling and turned to stare. Kate was mortified.

Finally Garth stopped. "So," he asked, "what did you think?" His ears were up and forward, eyebrows raised, a big grin on his face. Clearly he had no clue.

"Unbelievable," Kate managed.

She had to get away from him. "I, uh — I'm gonna be right back," she told him. "I need some . . . water! Some water! Okay? So I'll just — hold on."

She loped down the hill. Behind her, she could hear Garth starting to howl again. She ran faster, but the awful sound still filled her ears. Was there anywhere she could possibly go to get away from it?

Humphrey had shaken Lilly off and slunk down to a small stream near the base of the hill.

"Oh, he's not important," he muttered, mimicking Kate. "Just take little coyote Humphrey and run along. Humph!"

A rustling distracted him and he glanced up—to see Kate running toward him.

"Well, now!" Humphrey smiled.

Kate had almost reached the stream, and the awful howling had finally stopped. She glanced back to see Garth once more at the top of the hill, looking majestic. But that sound haunted her. She turned toward the stream again—

—and jumped as Humphrey appeared right in front of her.

"Ah!"

"Ah!" he mimicked her. Then he chuckled. "So where's Barf?"

"It's Garth," Kate corrected him primly. "And we're just . . . taking a little break."

"A break?" Humphrey studied her.

"What?" she demanded. "Is that so strange?"

"No, no," he assured her. "You kidding? I always like to take a break ten minutes into a howl."

"Well, so do I!" Kate started to walk away but Humphrey trotted alongside her.

"Your howling partner," he commented. "He's not a stud, is he? He's more like . . . it's like stud, but not. What is it, again? Um . . . oh, a dud! That's it. Isn't he?"

"No, he's not," Kate insisted, even though inside she was screaming, *Yes, he is!* "He's actually, um—"

"Strong?" Humphrey suggested.

"Yes, strong! And, uh—"

"Proud?"

"Yes! Proud! And he's, oh, what's the word I'm looking for? Um—"

"An Alpha's Alpha?" Humphrey offered.

"That's right," Kate agreed. "An Alpha's Alpha."

"Good thing, too," Humphrey commented.

"Because with a howl like that, if he was anything less he'd be unapproachable!"

"Oh!" Kate growled, realizing he'd been leading her on. "You get me so mad!"

Suddenly she felt something stab her. *Ow!* But the pain quickly changed to numbness as a wave of fuzzy warmth spread through her body.

"Hey, I was just kidding," Humphrey said, backing up a pace as she wobbled toward him. This was the first time she'd really looked at his face since she'd been back, and she smiled, feeling a bit light-headed.

"You're kinda cute," she mumbled.

"Really?" He broke into a big grin. "You think?" He said something else, but Kate couldn't really hear him over the sudden buzzing in her ears and behind her eyes. She stumbled.

"*Ow!*" Humphrey jerked as something sharp struck him. "These mosquitoes are out of control!"

Kate wasn't really listening anymore. "I'll meet you on Mars," she whispered. "Right after I eat the Milky Way." Then she collapsed.

"*Oooh*, sounds good," Humphrey agreed, his

words slurring together. "Save some for me." Then his legs folded and he toppled to the ground beside her.

Through the haze, Kate was vaguely aware of shapes and sounds approaching—like paws but heavier. Then something grabbed her and lifted her up. She was lowered down onto a flat, rough, cool surface that smelled of tree sap. Then something was placed above her, blocking out the moonlight, and she fell asleep.

# CHAPTER FOUR

**B**ang!

Kate woke to a sharp rap on the head. *"Ow!"* She tried to sit up, and bumped her head. "Hey!" Her eyes blinked open, but she couldn't see anything! After an instant's panic she realized there was a tiny bit of light filtering in through holes in whatever was on top of her, which felt like wood. More wood lay beneath her, and on all sides. She was closed in!

"Where am I?" she wondered out loud. There was a dull rumble all around her, and her rear ached. Then the world shifted and she bumped her head again. *"Ow!"* She scrambled to keep her balance as the ground tilted wildly, grating against something else, and finally settled at an angle.

"*Ooohhh . . .*" she heard from somewhere nearby. She recognized that voice!

"Humphrey, is that you?" she called.

"Kate?" he responded. It *was* him! "Where are we?" She could hear him moving and the sound of his nails against wood. He must be close.

"I don't know," she admitted.

"Oh." There was a pause. "Maybe we're dead."

The rumbling increased slightly, and Kate's surroundings shifted again, slamming into something else and sending her tumbling. "Ouch!" She complained as she fell. "*Ow!*"

Nearby, Humphrey was making similar noises.

"Nope, not dead," he decided after a second.

Kate shoved at the wood in front of her, then started swiping at it with her claws.

"Kate?" Humphrey asked. "What are you doing?"

"Trying to get out," she answered. She slammed her shoulder into the side, but all that did was rock her prison against something else and make it slam back into her again. Both she and Humphrey yelped in pain.

"Kate, whoa," he urged. "Calm down. Listen, maybe they're taking us to where there's more food."

"Or maybe we *are* the food," Kate replied.

"Oh, you're right!" She could hear the sudden realization—and fear—in his voice. "Fight, Kate! Fight, fight, fight!"

She struggled again, but it was no use. They were trapped!

After a while she grew tired and sank to her haunches to rest. . . . Then, suddenly, the rumbling around them stopped.

"What's happening?" Humphrey called out.

"I don't know," she told him. "But be ready. This could be our chance."

Her prison suddenly jerked and twisted, sending her flying. There was a strange sensation of movement all around, and then a dull thump and things settled again. A second thump nearby made her think Humphrey had just received the same treatment.

Next she heard a grating, ripping noise from right in front of her! Kate crouched and put her ears back, baring her fangs as she waited for whatever beast had made that noise. Then, with a sudden loud tear, the front of the prison was torn away. Daylight! Freedom!

Kate didn't waste any time. She bounded forward, out of the prison and into the open air. She spotted trees a short ways ahead, and made for them as fast as she could. She heard shuffling and then yelping and then pounding paws beside and a little behind her, and smiled. Humphrey was free as well! They'd figure out where they were and what had happened later. For now she just wanted to get well away from that prison! No one was confining her, ever again!

Humphrey shook his head and struggled to keep up with Kate. He'd risked a quick glance behind him as he'd taken off, and had seen several humans standing around a pair of strange wooden crates. Was that what they'd been trapped in?

It didn't matter. What mattered was that they were free. They were out, and soon they would be—

His thoughts skidded to a halt as he and Kate burst through the trees and onto a ridge. Spread out before them was a wide mountain range. It was beautiful. There was only one problem.

"This isn't Jasper!" Kate gasped.

Humphrey slid to a stop beside her and caught his breath. "Yeah," he agreed. He looked around. "But it sure is—" Then he saw something small and gray hurtling toward them. "Rock!"

Kate whirled around and spotted it as well. "Quick, get down!" She grabbed him and tugged him to the ground as the rock sailed past where his head had been. In an instant Kate was up and loping in the direction it had come from. Humphrey followed her, and a second later they were looking at the strangest thing they'd ever seen.

It was a small clearing a little ways ahead of and below them. Two birds were waddling around it. One, a goose, was holding a branch that widened at one end. He was waving that end at a rock sitting in front of him, looking like he was about to swat it. The other bird, a duck, followed behind him. He was carrying a bag made of vines and leaves across his back, and there were several other branches stuck in it. Three porcupines stood nearby, watching them intently.

"What are they doing?" Kate whispered.

"It looks like they're playing some sort of weird game," Humphrey whispered back. He was an expert on weird games.

"Maybe they can tell us how to get home."

Humphrey grinned. "Yeah, and if they can't, we can eat them." His stomach gurgled.

Kate shared his grin. "Yeah." She started toward them. "Follow my lead." Then she leaped up to a small cliff nearby and jumped off it, flipping in mid-air and landing perfectly on her feet.

Humphrey took off after her, but stumbled at the cliff's edge and landed hard. Fortunately Kate hadn't noticed.

"Right behind you," he mumbled, grimacing in pain as he limped after her.

The birds panicked when Kate and Humphrey appeared and loomed over them. Unfortunately, the goose's reaction to panic was to smack Humphrey on the nose with the branch and then take to the air. Humphrey managed to latch onto the goose's leg, but it wound up dragging him into the air along with it, where it scraped him against several trees, a few branches, a thorn bush, and even an idle moose before Humphrey's weight finally made it crash into some mud. The duck had been hurrying to keep up and Kate had kept pace behind it, so when the duck reached the goose Kate was able to pounce on them both.

"Okay," the goose said in a strange accent. Its bill stretched in a nervous smile. "You have a question?"

"Yeah," Kate agreed. She leaned in close. "Where are we?"

A few minutes later, she was still trying to process the answer.

"Idaho?"

"Idaho," the goose, Marcel, repeated. Kate had let him up and he was now washing the mud off in a water fountain he'd led them to. "Land of mountains, rivers, lakes . . . and a few billion potatoes."

"Sawtooth National Wilderness Park, to be precise," the duck, Paddy, added.

Kate shook her head. "What are we doing in Idaho?"

Paddy smirked. "You were relocated to repopulate."

What?! Kate glanced at Humphrey, who grinned at her, tail wagging with excitement.

"They want you big wolves to make a lot of little wolves," Marcel clarified, and he and Paddy chuckled.

"Sounds good to me," Humphrey agreed quickly. "A park shouldn't be without some wolves. I mean, it's for the good of the park, right?"

"No," Kate told him firmly. "We have to get home. Now. There's going to be trouble if I don't get back to Jasper."

"All right, all right," Humphrey told her. "You're freaking out."

"I'm not freaking out!" she snapped. "I just have to get home!"

He rolled his eyes. "Is this about Barf?"

"It's Garth," she reminded him pointedly, "and

it's about responsibilities. So I don't expect you to understand!" Which wasn't fair, really, but she was angry and worried. She remembered what Tony had told her father: "If we have to, we'll fight for the valley."

"Can you help me?" she asked Marcel. He was lying facedown on a table while Paddy ran up and down his back. "I need to get home—fast!"

"All right, Miss Fast. Where is home, sweet home?" the goose's voice was muffled by the table.

"Jasper Park, Canada."

That made Marcel take notice. "Jasper Park? Get out of here! We love Jasper Park!"

"Oh, yes," Paddy agreed. "We've toured it many times."

"Paddy, please," Marcel reprimanded him. He turned back to Kate and Humphrey. "We've toured it many times."

"So you can help me, then?" Kate demanded. "Get home?"

Paddy turned to Marcel. "We haven't played Jasper in quite a while. I think it would be a smash-

Humphrey and his friends logboarding.

Kate and the Alphas on the hunt.

Kate getting ready to meet
Garth for the moonlight howl.

Kate and Humphrey meet
Marcel in Iowa.

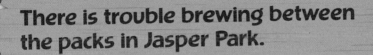

There is trouble brewing between the packs in Jasper Park.

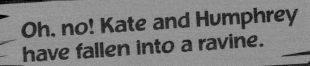

Oh, no! Kate and Humphrey have fallen into a ravine.

A daring rescue!

Humphrey makes friends
with a bear cub.

But the cub's mama is not happy about it!

Humphrey uses logboarding to save Kate and escape from the bear.

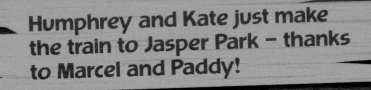

Humphrey and Kate just make the train to Jasper Park – thanks to Marcel and Paddy!

Welcome home!

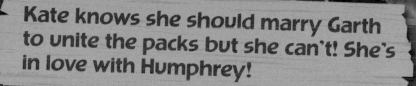

Kate knows she should marry Garth to unite the packs but she can't! She's in love with Humphrey!

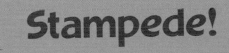

Stampede!

The packs unite and everyone is happy!

Kate and Humphrey get their happy ending after all.

ing idea!" They had already explained that the game they had been playing was called "golf," and that they played it all over the countryside.

"This is true," Marcel agreed. "So of course I will help." He smiled at Kate and Humphrey. "I like you two. You make me laugh, ha ha. And you didn't eat me, so I owe you a favor."

"Great. How do we get there?" Kate was ready to run—she just needed a direction.

Marcel sat up and shook his head. "You will never reach it on your own," he told her. "It is much too far. But I know a way." He hopped down off the table, and Paddy joined him with a flutter. "Come with me."

Kate stared. "What," she asked, "is that?"

Marcel smiled. He and Paddy had led her and Humphrey to the edge of the woods, where a small cabin stood. Next to it was something she recognized as a truck—sort of. The back end was huge, and had doors and windows like it was a tiny house on wheels. "This," he explained, using a golf club to open the back door, "is a truck camper. It's your ride home."

Paddy nodded. "Quick!" he urged. "Get in!"

Humphrey peered into the strange shell. "Boxed up twice in one day," he muttered. "What are the odds?"

All four of them turned as the cabin door creaked open.

"Hide!" Marcel and Paddy whispered. They all ducked around to the front of the strange vehicle as two humans emerged: a big, beefy man and a tiny woman. Both had gray hair and lined features but a spring in their step.

"Garn and Debbie Theakakis," Paddy explained quietly.

Marcel nodded. "Lucky for you, they travel to Jasper every year, right after Sawtooth."

The man, Garn, was carrying suitcases, which he set down by the camper's door. Then he turned and glanced around, taking a big, deep breath. "The day's looking pretty," he announced, his voice booming, as he opened the door and tossed the luggage inside, then turned back to Debbie, "and so is my woman!"

She covered her mouth as if to hide her smile. "Oh!"

The camper's radio was on, and a song began to play. Debbie's smile grew. "This is the song that was playing when we first met," she remembered out loud.

Garn grinned. "Come here, you!" He swept her into his arms. "Let's dance!"

"He was in a motorcycle gang," Marcel told the wolves as they all scurried beneath the camper to avoid the human couple now dancing around it. "She was a librarian."

"Yes, it's like opposites attract, if you will." Paddy eyed Kate and Humphrey knowingly, making Humphrey stifle a laugh and Kate look away.

Humphrey was enjoying the music, but Kate was all business. "We have to get in," she reminded him, and led the way out from under the camper, around the side, and to the back door. She was just opening her mouth to grab the door handle between her teeth when Garn and Debbie twirled back toward them!

There was nowhere to hide! Humphrey watched them carefully and had an idea. It was their only chance.

"Do what they're doing," he whispered to Kate, and stepped into Garn's immense shadow. Kate understood right away and joined him, moving in Debbie's wake. They copied the human couple's dance moves exactly, and managed to stay just outside their field of vision. And, Kate had to admit to herself, it was kind of fun!

Finally, however, she found herself next to the camper again. She leaped for the back door but it swung open at her touch, throwing her backward— fortunately Humphrey caught her, dipping her smoothly as the music ended. Garn was doing the same to Debbie.

"I love ya, Deb," the big man was saying to his wife. Humphrey grinned at Kate. She shoved him away. Garn walked Debbie around to her side of the truck and held the door for her, then closed it and walked around the front to reach the driver's side.

"Get inside now!" Marcel hissed at them. "Very quick!"

Kate jumped in immediately. Humphrey hesitated, and the truck roared to life, then started rolling away! But Humphrey was quick on his feet and took off after it.

"Oh well," he said to himself. "Back in a box!" Then he dove for the door and slid inside.

"Good luck, you two!" Paddy called down to them. He and Marcel were flying behind the camper.

"We will be watching out for you from above!"

"Thanks!" Humphrey called back. "See you in Jasper!" He slid the door shut and checked out the camper's interior. The couple's luggage was right behind him, and other odds and ends lay strewn about the room. While Kate laid her head on her paws and dozed, Humphrey explored. He found an old biker's helmet and a pair of sunglasses, and put them on at once. Up front, Garn had turned up the radio. Humphrey listened to the music, tail wagging in time. Now this was traveling in style!

# CHAPTER FIVE

Kate woke up some time later, feeling the truck slow to a stop. She stretched. She blinked—and wondered why the world seemed so dark. And what was on her head?

Standing up and shaking off, she dislodged a pair of sunglasses and a helmet. Humphrey! She turned toward him, ready to snap at him for being so idiotic, but the words disappeared. He was hopping around.

"What's wrong with you?" she asked, concern overriding the anger.

"I have to go," Humphrey whined. Oh.

"You can't leave," she reminded him. "Can't you hold it?"

He stared piteously at her.

"Well, did you try crossing your legs?"

He nodded and jerked around in a circle. His legs were already crossed tightly.

"Holding your breath?"

"Yes! I almost passed out!" She started to suggest closing his eyes but Humphrey cut her off. "In or out," he told her. "I *am* going!"

She sighed but stepped aside as he made for the camper door. "Hurry up!" she urged him, but he shushed her.

"I can't go when I feel pressured!" He slipped out. They had pulled up at some sort of truck stop, and Humphrey made a beeline for a cluster of trash bins off to the side,

Back in Jasper Park, Lilly was showing Garth around the western pack's territory. She'd claimed it was the least she could do, since her sister had been the one to stand him up. The truth was, she had just wanted some way to spend time with the big eastern pack wolf. He was so strong and handsome!

"So why is this called Rabbit Poo Mountain?" he

asked as they stepped out onto a short, rounded hill.

"Because this is where rabbits like to poo," she answered. He made a disgusted face at that and began walking on the tips of his paws, trying not to touch the ground any more than he had to. Lilly couldn't help giggling. "I was just kidding," she admitted after a second.

"Oh." Garth relaxed and studied her. "I get it. You're a funny Omega." When she nodded, he raised one brow. "Okay, make me laugh."

Now Lilly felt nervous. She was good at getting Kate to laugh, but how would she amuse this strapping wolf?

"Um, well . . . I can do impressions," she said finally. She twisted herself around, putting her back to the ground and contorting so all four paws were waving in the air. "What's this?" she asked him.

"Got me," Garth answered.

"It's a turtle that fell and can't get up."

He didn't say anything for a second, and she glanced over at him to find a look she didn't recognize on his face. Was that—was that respect?

"That's pretty good," he told her.

Pleased by the compliment, Lilly tried another one. This time she spread herself flat on the ground, limbs splayed out. "Okay, what's this?"

"*Uhhh . . .*"

"It's turtle roadkill."

This time Garth laughed. Lilly felt a thrill shoot through her. She was hanging out with a hot Alpha, and he thought she was funny!

"What else can you do?" he asked as she pulled herself back up.

Lilly hung her head. "I just do turtles."

She thought he'd walk away then. Instead he surprised her. "It's my turn. You wanna see something an Alpha can do?"

"*Uhhh. . . .*" Lilly wasn't sure how to respond. A male had never asked her to do anything with him before! "Would my mother approve?" She couldn't believe she'd just asked that!

But Garth grinned at her. He was so good-looking! "Of course."

She managed a shy smile. "Well, okay then." He

turned toward a dirt path and she followed him, wondering at the strange jolt she felt every time he looked at her. And, she wondered, did he feel it, too?

Ah, that was better! Humphrey shook himself and trotted back toward the camper. As he sidled past the trash bins, however, his nose began to twitch. What was that wonderful smell?

Glancing around, he spotted a bag between the bins. The smell was coming from there!

Humphrey nudged the bag with his nose and pulled it apart with his teeth. Inside were several round lumps, a bit like squat toadstools in shape but covered in something soft and sweet. Hmm!

Kate frowned. What was he doing? An RV had pulled in between the camper and the trash, blocking her view. But Humphrey should have been back by now!

Humphrey glanced up as the RV parked near him. A chubby boy was sitting in the back, eating—whatever this thing was Humphrey had just found! The boy's face was smeared with the sweet covering, and he looked thoroughly pleased with himself. A sturdy little dog next to him was jumping up and down with excitement.

The boy looked out and saw Humphrey. They locked eyes. Then the boy noticed the things Humphrey had found, and smiled. He held up one like it and took a big bite. So Humphrey nudged one of his loose and took a big bite. Yum! It was amazing!

He lifted his head and grinned at the boy. The boy responded by balancing his treat on his head for a second, then tilting his head back so it slid down his forehead and onto his nose!

*Oh yeah?* Humphrey thought. He balanced one on his nose—and then tossed it up and caught in his mouth, chomping into it and then swallowing it. *Top that!*

The boy tried getting his cupcake to go from his nose to his mouth, but it fell off instead. Ha, take that, human!

Kate started to panic as she saw Garn and Debbie. They had apparently gone into the truck stop, because now they were coming back out! She craned her neck, trying to see around the RV as Garn held Debbie's door for her and she hopped inside. Where was Humphrey?

Enough playing around, Humphrey decided. He waved to the boy and turned to go around the RV—when a light came on near the back of the truck stop. What now?

A door opened and a human stepped out carrying two large, smelly bags. More trash! He was heading straight for the trash bins, and stopped dead when he saw Humphrey standing there, not ten feet away.

The human took one look at Humphrey, then dropped the bags and began backing away. "Help!" he shouted. "It's a rabid wolf! Max, bring that gun!"

Rabid? Humphrey knew what that meant, but why would this human think he was rabid? Then he realized there was something sticky across his muzzle. He licked at it. Oh, the sweet covering. Tasty! But maybe it looked like . . .

"No," he told the human. "No, I'm not rabid. It's

food! See!" He licked more of it off. But the human was still backing away and screaming.

The RV drove away, and Humphrey twisted around. He could see Kate in the camper, staring at him. Then her eyes flicked past him, and he turned back to see a second human approaching. And he had a gun!

"This is it for you, wolf," the human announced, aiming at Humphrey. "Any last wishes?"

Oh, great! Now what was he going to do? Humphrey looked for a way to distract the human—and thought of it. He took a half-step forward—and peed on the man's feet.

"*Ewww!*" the human complained, jumping back.

Humphrey laughed, but his chuckle was drowned out by another noise: the rumble of the camper's engine. Oh, no! It was pulling out—and Kate was still in the back!

And the human was back in his face again, gun pointing right at his head. Now he was angry, too!

Suddenly a brown blur leaped onto the human, knocking him to the ground. Kate!

Humphrey didn't hesitate. The camper was too far away for him to reach, so he bolted toward the back of the truck stop's parking lot. Kate was next to him a second later. Then a tall, metal fence came into view.

"We're trapped!" Humphrey wailed.

He glanced over his shoulder. The human was back on his feet, the gun aimed at them again!

"Duck!" Humphrey yelled to Kate. Both of them dove to the side as the gun went off.

*Boom!*

It blew a huge hole in the metal fence. Yes!

Kate raced through it, with Humphrey right behind her. Man, whatever those sweet things were, eating them was dangerous!

Unfortunately, the camper was now out of reach. They watched from the woods as it drove onto the interstate and picked up speed. An instant later it had vanished from view.

Kate was clearly furious. She turned and stalked off without a word. Humphrey followed her, tail between his legs. Could the day get any worse?

*Boom!* Thunder crashed nearby, and then lightning flashed through the sky. Rain began to fall all around.

Great.

"Okay," Humphrey said after a minute. "Thinking with my belly instead of my head, not a good idea. I get it. I say we build a comfy den—"

Kate cut him off. "I'm going home."

"I know that," he told her. "We both are. But right now it's raining."

"I'm not stopping."

He sighed. Swell. Then he started doing a little dance. "Rain, rain, go away," he sang. "Get outta here, rain. No one wants you around."

Kate glared at him. "What are you doing?"

"It's a rain dance," he informed her. "To stop it from raining." He continued dancing. "Because you're all wet and it's gonna ruin our day."

Kate snorted. "Rain dances . . . make it rain," she pointed out.

"Oh." Humphrey stopped and considered. "Well, I'll just do it backwards!" He started both the moves and the word in reverse, determined to get a laugh out of her—

—and it stopped raining!

"Wow," Humphrey said softly. "That actually worked!'

Then a torrent of water dumped onto him from the leaves above, completely soaking him.

"Or maybe not." He turned toward Kate, but she was already vanishing into the woods. Great. Shaking off as much of the water as he could, Humphrey took off after her.

Later that night, Kate reached a long ridge. It looked out over a steep ravine, with a creek running through the middle. She didn't see any way around it, so she started working her way down the side, but the ground was soaked and slippery. She reached the bottom a bit more quickly than she had planned but shook it off and, finding a suitable rock, launched herself over the creek. It was running fast, swollen from the storm, but she cleared it easily. Then she took a deep breath and started up the other side.

Climbing back up was a lot harder, though. She was halfway when her paws began to slip and she started sliding back down toward the creek. No!

Humphrey had reached the ridge in time to see Kate sliding down on the other side. "Hold on, Kate!" he yelled. "I'm coming!" Glancing around, he spotted a long vine hanging across the ravine. Perfect! He leaped for it and caught it in his mouth and paws, his momentum swinging him out over the creek.

"Ah-ah-ah, ah-ah!" he hollered. Kate turned and stared at him. What was he doing? He was crazy! What kind of wolf swung from a vine?

Apparently, Humphrey did. He swung toward Kate, ready to rescue her—

—and groaned as he began to slow, the swings becoming smaller, until he finally stalled to a stop. Right over the creek.

"Don't worry," he assured Kate through clenched teeth. "This is all part of the plan."

"I can see that," she replied. Then her paws slipped again, and she cried out.

Humphrey reached up and took a firmer grip on the vine with his jaws, clamping them shut to make sure he wouldn't pull loose. Then he let the rest of his body hang down. "Kate!" he called to her. "Grab my tail!"

"Grab your what?"

He sighed. "Take those big Alpha jaws," he instructed, "and grab my—*aaaahhh!*" That last part was because she had done as he'd said, and her teeth were now locked onto his tail. "*Aaggh*, my tail! My tail!" He took a breath and forced himself to work past the pain. "Now wiggle."

She didn't move, but he was sure she was staring at him with that puzzled look of hers.

"Wiggle around!" he hissed at her through teeth still clamped onto the vine.

Obediently she began to wiggle, making the vine swing slightly. Realizing what he intended, Kate put more force into it, swinging wider and wider. Unfortunately, each movement also tore at Humphrey's tail more and more, sending fresh jolts of pain up it and into his body. But he wrapped his paws back around the vine and added his strength and weight to Kate's, increasing their swing further. Then he heaved with his tail, whipping it forward—and sending Kate flying onto the other side of the ravine!

Yes!

Then Humphrey couldn't hold on anymore.

Kate flew to the other side and landed hard, knocking the wind out of her. After a second she shook her head, took a deep breath, and looked around. Where was Humphrey?

She saw the vine—but it was broken off! No!

"Oh, no! Humphrey!" Kate look around frantically. *Please be okay*, she thought desperately. *Please!*

"Whatcha lookin' for?" Humphrey asked. "Come on, let's get to some shelter."

Kate studied him for a second. He had saved her life! Even though she'd been mad at him, and had tried to leave him behind, he'd risked his own life to save her.

"Yeah," she said. "Okay."

# CHAPTER SIX

**H**umphrey woke the next morning and stretched. The little den they'd fashioned last night was warm and dry, and he felt comfortable, cozy, and rested. He blinked, rolled over, blinked again, and smiled. He and Kate had curled up on opposite sides of the den, but now he was lying right beside her, their noses almost touching. As he watched, her eyes flickered, then opened. She didn't startle when she saw him there beside her, however—and was that the hint of a smile on her face?

"Fore!"

Both of them started at the voice, which had come from somewhere nearby—and started more when a small rock landed between them.

"Well, well, well, what do we have here?" Marcel asked, fluttering to the den's entrance.

"Oh, I say," Paddy commented, waddling up. "We caught them at quite the bad time."

"No, we caught them at a good time," Marcel corrected, and both birds laughed.

Kate's half-smile had faded to a scowl at the birds' appearance, and it was still in place as she hauled herself to her feet.

"What are you doing here?" she asked them.

Marcel refused to be cowed. "No, the question is what are *you* doing here?" he replied. "I give you a first-class ticket home—"

"Yes," Paddy interrupted. "A straight shot, right to the pin—"

"And you blow it!"

"Over a cupcake," Paddy pointed out. Humphrey filed that name away for later.

"There has to be another way for us to get to Jasper," Kate insisted.

Marcel fluttered his wings. "Another way? What am I, a travel agent?"

Humphrey could see it was time to turn on the old Omega charm again. "Come on," he told Marcel. "Are you kidding me? A great sportsman like yourself always knows a few ways to win a game, am I right?"

Marcel smiled. "Well," he admitted, "there could be a train." He snagged one of the golf-club sticks from Paddy's bag and took a practice swing.

"Actually, there is a train," Paddy corrected. "It's the Canadian Express."

"Paddy, please," Marcel scolded him. Then he turned back to Kate and Humphrey. "It's called the Canadian Express."

Paddy didn't seem too fazed by Marcel's rebuke. "Yes, it shoots right by Jasper Park."

"Right by Jasper Park," Marcel agreed. "If you can catch it—"

"You will be home in no time," Paddy finished for him.

Kate nodded. "Great! So where do we board?"

That got a honking laugh from Marcel.

Paddy gestured toward at the base of a nearby

mountain. "On the other side of that mountain," he explained.

"Wow," Lilly whispered. Garth had just demonstrated a hunting move he'd invented. "You're good."

"Thanks!" He seemed happy for the compliment. "Now you try it."

"Oh, no," she protested. "I'm not much of a hunter."

"Come on, you'll do great. Just do what I do." He coached her on what to do, and she did her best to copy his moves, but she was so thrilled to be near him she couldn't concentrate. And she wasn't an Alpha anyway—she just didn't have the skills. So while he leaped and caught the branch he'd imagined as his prey, she sailed past him—right into a patch of tall grass.

"*Oof!*" Lilly hit the ground hard and rolled— right into a hollowed-out log. Oh, great! Perfect! She stood up, but the log was wedged onto her back and she stumbled, trying to shake it loose.

"Lilly?" Garth rushed over to her. He actually

sounded concerned, but when he saw her he stopped and laughed. Lilly tried to blink away her tears. She must look ridiculous!

But his laughter didn't sound mean. "A turtle, right?" he asked after a second. "Nice one!" He sounded like he meant it, but Lilly still felt like an idiot.

"I told you I was no good," she mumbled.

Garth flipped the log off her back. "Maybe this will help," he said gently . . . and reached up to tug the hair out of her eyes. Then he stared. "Wow."

Lilly wasn't sure what he meant. "Wow what?"

"Your eyes," Garth whispered, still staring. "They're beautiful!"

Lilly froze. She couldn't believe what she'd just heard, and she didn't want to lose this moment. Not ever.

After a second Garth glanced away. "Come on, let's try again," he suggested. He turned away, but glanced back. "Are you coming?"

"Oh, yeah," she replied quickly, trotting after him. "Yeah." Her hair fell over her eyes again, and she paused to blow it back out of the way, a happy little smile on her lips.

In Jasper Park all the snow had melted, but here in Sawtooth there was still some winter left. Kate and Humphrey had both been surprised to find snow. Something about the smooth white slopes lifted both their spirits, and Kate found herself calling to Humphrey, "I'll race you to the top!"

"You're on!" he replied, and they both ran for it. Kate laughed from the pure exhilaration of speed.

"Give it up, Humphrey!" she shouted. "You'll never beat me!" When he didn't make a clever reply she turned. "Humphrey?" But no one was there. Now where had he gone this time?

*Whack!*

A snowball hit her in the back of the head. Kate shook it off and swiveled back around, just in time to see Humphrey jump out from behind a tree a little way ahead of her. That sneak!

"Ha!" he shouted. "Omega one, Alpha zero."

"Oh, really?" Kate put her tail to him and crouched down, then started digging with her hind legs. They tore up the snow, sending a flurry of snowballs speeding down the mountain—straight at Humphrey.

*Whomp!*

"Okay, enough!" he screamed, cowering under the onslaught. "I get it!"

Kate laughed.

Humphrey shoved aside the snowballs surrounding him and grinned at her. "Well, look who's having fun," he commented.

Kate stopped mid-laugh. He was right—she was having fun. But she couldn't tell him that. And she had her duty to think of. That came first. "I should go check on the train," she said, and made her way past him up the hill.

"Wait!" Humphrey called out behind her. But Kate didn't look back.

Not until she heard the giggling.

Humphrey heard it too. Someone was giggling, and it was right . . . there!

He whirled around and found himself looking at a little bear cub. "Hey there," he said softly.

"What are you?" the cub asked him.

"Me? Well, I'm a wolf."

"I've never met a wolf," the cub explained. "You're really strange."

"Oh, I am, am I?" Humphrey made a funny face, and the cub giggled again.

"You're totally weird," it said.

Humphrey laughed and playfully lunged at the cub. It squealed and ran away, now laughing openly. Humphrey chased after it, deliberately sliding past it and half falling. It was a cute little thing, and it was nice to make somebody laugh again—especially somebody who didn't feel guilty about it afterward.

He didn't notice that Kate had paused to watch him for a minute. Nor did he see the tender look in her eyes as she admired the way he played with the bear cub. . . .

After a minute the cub got tired and stopped running, so Humphrey stopped as well. He got an idea, and scooped up some snow. "You asked for it," he said, and tossed it gently. It landed right on the cub's head and fell apart, showering the little bear with snow. But apparently that was too much for the cub, and it started to cry.

"Oh, hey, it's okay," Humphrey told it, hurrying over and patting it on the head. "I'm really sorry. It's okay." He glanced around, but Kate had apparently continued on. At least she hadn't seen him make a tiny little bear cub cry.

The cub was still crying, and he kept trying to calm it down, but nothing worked . . . until suddenly the cub stopped sobbing. Then it started giggling. Huh?

He turned around to find a huge, angry bear charging toward him. Humphrey immediately guessed it was the cub's mom. He knew there was no talking his way out of this one—so he simply turned tail and ran.

He hoped the train was on its way!

Kate slowed to a stop at the top of the mountain. There, off in the distance, she saw a plume of smoke snaking its way around a hill. That had to be the train!

She turned to call out to Humphrey, and—
*wham!* He ran right into her!

"What's wrong with you?" Kate asked as she
picked herself up again. His eyes were wild and his
fur was a mess.

"That!" he answered as a huge mother bear
emerged from the trees.

*Oh great, what has he gone and done this time?*
Kate wondered as she crouched and put her ears
back, baring her fangs.

"Don't move," she warned him quietly. "We can
handle this."

"We can?" Humphrey's question became a lot
more worrying a second later when another bear
emerged to their right—and then a third appeared
behind them. They were surrounded!

"Okay," Kate admitted as all three bears rose on
their hind legs and roared. "Now we're in trouble."

Humphrey tried telling jokes, but one of the bears
simply slapped him aside, sending him crashing into
a nearby boulder. The sight of her friend being hurt
sent Kate into a rage. She leaped up, clawing at one

bear's leg, hopping onto another's back, clawing the third in the face. She was everywhere at once. Then one of them swatted her down, and she fell to the ground.

"Kate!" All at once Humphrey was on the bear's head, then back on the ground and nudging her to her feet. "Get up!" He helped her stand, but the bears were closing in, pushing them toward the edge of the cliff.

A log hung there, teetering over the edge, and Kate and Humphrey found themselves being backed up onto the log itself. One of the bears started slamming and shaking the log, and it cracked at that end.

"Good luck joking your way out of this one," Kate muttered to Humphrey. To her surprise, he winked at her. Then the bear clambered onto the log and it broke under the added weight, sending Kate, Humphrey, and the bear all tumbling over the side.

*"Aaaahhh!"*

They crashed onto the slope below, their fall cushioned by the snow. Humphrey saw the log rolling toward him and ducked as it flipped overhead and smashed into a nearby tree, shattering into pieces. One of those pieces slid near him, and he instinctively hopped onto it. At once those months of logboarding kicked in.

The bear swiped at Humphrey but he slid past it, then swooped down alongside Kate.

"Hey," he called out. "Need a ride?" The bear had caught up, and maneuvered between them. "Jump!" Humphrey told Kate. "Trust me!"

Apparently she did, because she immediately leaped onto the bear's back and from there onto the log, landing right next to Humphrey. He smiled.

The bear hadn't given up, and lunged at them again. "Angle left," Humphrey directed, showing Kate how to move her paws on the log. She did, and the log slid left away from the bear. But now they were heading straight toward some boulders. "Roll right!" Kate did, and they careened past the boulder. "Yes!"

The bear lurched up alongside them, rearing back for one more swipe. Then it suddenly paused, a look of horror appearing on its face.

"Why are you looking at me like that?" Humphrey demanded.

In response, the bear pointed ahead of them. The slope ended in a jutting edge like a ramp . . . right over an embankment. And below the embankment rolled the train!

"*Aaahh!*" Humphrey, Kate, and the bear all screamed as they hurtled off the ramp and into the air. The bear sailed right over the train, smashing to the ground on the other side. The log slammed into the train, shattering into kindling. And Kate and Humphrey sailed neatly through an open boxcar door, right into a pile of straw. *Whoomph!*

"Now that," Humphrey declared as he shook off straw and clambered to his feet, "was a ride!"

# CHAPTER SEVEN

**N**ight had fallen. Kate and Humphrey stared out the boxcar's open door as wilderness sped past on either side. They were both excited, and still a bit giddy from their recent close call.

"I can't believe you threw a snowball at me!" Kate blurted out, laughing at the memory of the face he'd made.

"Me?" Humphrey laughed with her. "What about you, with all those snowballs? It was like my own personal avalanche!"

"And you with that little bear, and the snowball fight," Kate remembered. "It was so cute!"

"Yeah, her mama didn't think so," Humphrey

pointed out, but he was laughing, too. He swiped at the air, pretending to be the mama bear.

"But then you, with the log!" Kate skipped and slid and swished from side to side, as if she were still logboarding.

"Oh, the look on your face was so good!" Humphrey told her. "And then we—" he gestured at the open door, and pantomimed flying through it.

"Whoa!" they both shouted at the same time. Then they collapsed on the floor, writhing with laughter.

After a second Humphrey hitched himself up so he was leaning with his back against the wall next to the door. "You know," he said, "we make a pretty good team. Kate and Humphrey, world adventurers. What do you think?"

Kate moved up and sat beside him. "I think you're crazy." But she was smiling when she said it.

"You think I'm crazy? No." Humphrey shook his head. "I'm telling you, we're on to something here." He grinned at her. "Stick with me, pup—we'll go places."

Kate laughed. "I'll keep that in mind."

A cool silvery light shone through the door, and Humphrey pushed away from the wall and twisted around to see it. The full moon had risen. It was beautiful.

Humphrey couldn't help himself. He tilted his head back, raised his muzzle to the sky, opened his mouth, and began to howl.

"Humphrey?" Kate sidled over to join him. "What are you doing?"

With a start, Humphrey remembered where they were, where they were going—and why. "Oh, sorry," he muttered. "The moon, the moment, I just thought . . ." Then, in a sudden burst of courage, he decided to go for it. "Oh, come on, Kate!" he urged her. "Howl at the moon with me!"

Casting all caution to the winds, he began to howl again, putting his heart and soul into it.

Kate was taken aback. She hadn't expected Humphrey to howl—or for him to sound so good! His voice was amazing, and it sent chills through her. And thrills as well. Something about the sound, and about the obvious emotion in it, touched her deeply.

She couldn't resist. She tilted her own head back and raised her voice to join his.

Their two howls wound together, mixing to form a single rich, complex sound that encompassed them both. They were in perfect harmony, and Kate felt all her fears and doubts wash away. This was where she belonged—and who she belonged with.

Humphrey was thrilled. His heart beat faster as Kate's melody harmonized with his, and he closed his eyes, letting the song wash over him. He never wanted it to end.

Garth was howling, too—and it was so awful a bird toppled from a nearby tree, dead.

He sighed. "I know; it's not very good, is it?" His admission surprised Lilly, who was sitting beside him. It was the first time she'd heard him admit doubt about anything.

"No, it's not," she agreed gently. "But it could be." She stood and moved to stand in front of him. "Take a deep breath," she instructed. "And howl from right here—" She pressed one paw to his chest, right over his heart, and they both started slightly as their eyes met. There was no denying the energy that had just coursed between them, and Lilly smiled, seeing him answer her with a warm look of his own. "And I'll join in."

Garth nodded, unable to speak. Then he tilted his head back and howled. What a difference! Before it had been more of a growl, rough and uneven. Now it was a proper howl, still deep and strong, but smooth as well.

Lilly listened for a second, then joined in, her voice softer and sweeter. Her howl danced around his, and the two wove together, in perfect harmony. It was wonderful!

Afterward, Garth and Lilly frolicked together. He was so excited about his new ability! And when he looked at her, his eyes shone with something she'd seen every time her father looked at her mother. Was this love?

Then he stopped suddenly, ears swiveling around. Lilly wasn't sure what had happened, but all at once

Garth was crouched, lips pulled back, all business.

"You'd better go," he warned her in a low voice. He wouldn't even look at her!

"But . . ." Lilly was confused by his sudden change. "No one has to know."

"Please," he whispered. "Go. Now." He did glance at her finally, and she still saw the same glow there, but now there was something along with it. Desperation? Fear?

Lilly started to ask him to explain, but just then a bush nearby rustled. Its branches parted, and a large, graying wolf stalked forward. It was Garth's father, Tony, the eastern pack leader!

Lilly glanced around and realized the woods were dotted with eyes. Dozens of them! Now she understood—Garth hadn't been angry with her. He'd been worried about her!

She took off running. She had to find her father. The eastern pack was coming!

"*Bonjour*, my furry friend!"

Humphrey glanced up toward the boxcar door. It

was morning already. Kate was still asleep in a pile of hay nearby, and he padded to the door as quietly as he could, determined to let her sleep as long as possible.

Marcel and Paddy were flying alongside the train. "Are you guys crazy?" he asked.

"Well, that's up for debate," Paddy admitted, his wings beating furiously.

"And where is *mademoiselle*?" Marcel asked.

"She's sleeping. So be quiet." Humphrey eyed the two birds. "What are you guys doing here?

"Making sure you don't forget the run of the course," Paddy answered. His words didn't make much sense to Humphrey.

"Jasper Park," Marcel explained. "It is just a few miles up. Do not miss it!"

Humphrey nodded. "Jasper. Few miles. Got it."

"Good."

Paddy studied Kate. "I have to say," he commented, "your girlfriend looks quite pretty when she sleeps."

Humphrey sighed. "She's not my girlfriend."

*Bam!* A billboard came into view right next to the train, and the birds both slammed into it.

"You should work on that!" Marcel shouted as the train sped on, leaving him and Paddy behind.

"Yeah, I should." Humphrey sighed. He padded over to Kate and nudged her gently. "Kate," he said softly. "Wake up, Kate. Wake up."

Kate stirred, saw him, and smiled. Humphrey's heart skipped a beat. "Humphrey? Where are we?"

"We're—" Humphrey almost couldn't bear to say it. "We're back in Jasper."

"Oh." Kate hauled herself to her feet and glanced out the open door. "Well, we're home." Part of her was pleased, of course. But part of her had hoped this moment would never come.

"Yep. We're home." Humphrey sounded glum as well.

Both of them started to speak at the same time, and they smiled at each other.

"Please, you first," Humphrey insisted.

Kate looked down at her paws and shuffled them on the boxcar floor. "Humphrey," she started, "I just wanted to tell you, these past couple of days—they've been kind of fun. You've been . . . kind of fun." That wasn't what she'd wanted to say, but she was too embarrassed to admit the true depth of her feelings for him.

Humphrey seemed pleased, however. "Well, that's great," he said. "I told you we make a pretty good team."

The memory of them howling together brought a smile to Kate's face. "We do," she agreed.

"Well, I just wanted to tell you—" Humphrey started, but he sounded so earnest Kate interrupted.

"No, no, don't tell me." She rested a paw on his, then flushed. She wanted him to say something, but she couldn't bear it if he actually did. Not now, when they were almost home again—and when she still had her responsibility to the pack. But seeing the hurt in his eyes, she mustered up a laugh. "You have to go to the bathroom again?"

Humphrey looked relieved, and chuckled, playing along. "Why, do you see a truck stop?" But then he turned serious again. "No, I just wanted to tell you that I—"

Kate glanced up at him—and froze. Just beyond him, through the boxcar door, she saw their valley. And the eastern pack wolves lined up along one side of the valley wall. That could only mean one thing: war!

"Oh, no!" she said and gasped. She brushed past Humphrey and leaped off the train.

"Ah, geez." Humphrey shook his head, spun on his hind legs, and jumped out after her.

# CHAPTER EIGHT

**K**ate raced toward the valley. A part of her wished she'd stayed on that train and heard what Humphrey had to say. But right now she had other concerns.

As she sped across the familiar ground she saw more wolves along the valley wall. All of them were Alphas. And the western wall was just as crowded—with western pack wolves. It really was war!

She headed straight for a summit she knew. It was a favorite lookout point because it gave a full view of the entire length of the valley.

Another wolf moved alongside her, and she shied away instinctively before realizing who it was.

Humphrey! He'd followed her! Whatever his reasons, she was glad for his company.

She had almost reached the summit now, and she could see her father standing in front of their pack on the west side—and Tony before his pack on the east.

"It's a full moon, Winston," Tony called out.

"I can see that, Tony," Kate's father replied. Even from here Kate could tell he wasn't happy about the situation, but he stood firm.

"I didn't want it to come to this," Tony announced.

Winston didn't sound convinced when he replied, "But here we are."

Kate shook her head and slowed to make her way through the tricky last few yards to the top.

Tony was talking again. "All we asked was that you follow our customs," he insisted. "Unite the packs." There was a lot of nodding—on both sides. "But no—your daughter had to up and run away!"

That did it. "I didn't run away!" Kate shouted, scrambling to the very tip of the summit.

"Kate!" She had rarely heard such relief or delight

in her father's voice. He raced down into the valley, the rest of the pack right behind him. Kate ran down to meet him.

But Winston didn't reach her first. Eve burst out in front of him and covered the distance in a gold streak, almost barreling Kate down as she hugged her fiercely.

"We were so worried," Eve whispered, and Kate was touched.

"Where have you been?" Winston demanded after he, too, hugged her.

"In Idaho," Kate answered. "We were taken by the humans to another park."

Humphrey had just joined them. "We were supposed to repopulate," he added, grinning.

In a flash his laugh changed to a gurgle as Eve lunged forward and grabbed him by the throat.

"No, Mom!" Kate stepped forward to stop her. "We didn't repopulate. Humphrey actually helped me get home."

Eve dropped Humphrey immediately and smiled down at him.

"What a nice boy," she commented, turning her tail toward him and nuzzling Kate again.

Kate smiled and turned to her father. "I came back—"

"You came back to marry Garth," Tony announced, cutting her off as he and Garth and the rest of the eastern pack reached them.

Kate looked at Garth, who gave her an awkward smile. They both knew what had to be done.

"Yes," Kate agreed loudly. "I came back to marry Garth and unite the packs!"

Everyone howled with excitement, and she saw both Tony and Winston relax and beam at each other. Then she made the mistake of glancing at Humphrey, and felt her own heart break at the hurt reflected in his gaze.

"Marry?" he gasped out, still rubbing his throat. "You're getting married?"

"Yes." She did her best to sound thrilled. "No more fighting during hunts. No more scraps and bones at dinnertime. We're going to unite the packs!" She hoped she sounded convincing.

A group of female wolves descended upon her, showering her with congratulations, well wishes, and compliments. They dragged her away to help her prepare for the big event, and Kate let them. She couldn't bear to look at Humphrey again. She was an Alpha, and she had a duty. What her heart wanted didn't enter into it.

Humphrey stared as Kate disappeared into the pack of female wolves. He was still stunned. She was getting married? After everything they'd shared? He hadn't dared to hope she loved him, but he thought she'd felt something! He was sure of it!

A trio of gray bodies cut off his reverie. Then he felt himself being embraced.

"Welcome back, Humphrey," Salty told him.

"Good job bringing her home," Shakey added.

Mooch didn't say anything; he just hugged Humphrey tight.

Then the three of them began howling around him. They tried to lift him onto their backs, but collapsed into a wolf pile instead, laughing. Humphrey did his best to smile and laugh with them. But he couldn't help wishing he and Kate had never gotten off that train.

The next morning, Lilly helped Kate get ready. From where they sat overlooking the valley, Kate could see eastern and western wolves streaming into the valley. "Wow, big crowd," she muttered, trying to control her queasiness.

"Yeah, good times," her sister replied. The two of them had shared a tender reunion, but ever since then Lilly had been even less talkative than usual, and far glummer. It wasn't like her. There was something else different, too, but Kate couldn't figure out what.

"So what happened while I was gone?" she asked, trying to keep their conversation going.

"Not much."

Kate tried again. "I hear you and Garth spent some time together."

Just then Lilly tugged a little too hard at Kate's coat, eliciting an "Ow!" from her and a quick apology from Lilly.

"So what's he like?" Kate asked. "I'm sure he's perfect marrying material, right?"

*Crunch!* Lilly bit down on the pinecone, shattering it, and spat out the pieces.

"Well, if you like that sort of thing," she replied bitterly. "Big, brawny, and perfect." Kate twisted around to study her sister — and realized what else was different.

"Lilly, you're wearing your fur back!" It was true — Lilly had always let her forelock hang over her eyes, but now it was swept back. Kate could see her eyes, and how they were suddenly filling with tears.

"Sorry, I know," Lilly muttered, clawing the fur down and then darting away.

"But I liked it," Kate called after her. Her sister's behavior was confusing her.

Wondering about it was set aside, however, when a small round stone landed at her feet, rolling to her front left paw.

"Right on the pin," a familiar accented voice announced. Kate glanced up to see Marcel and Paddy alighting a few yards away. She ran over to hug them.

"I'm so happy to see you two," Kate told them.

"Well, we flew in to see that you made it home," Paddy admitted.

"And what do we find?" Marcel spread his wings to indicate the valley below. "*Voila!* You're getting married!"

"Yeah, I'm getting married," Kate agreed. The reunion turned awkward. "So, who told you?"

"I did."

Kate turned to see Humphrey striding toward them.

"Well, we should be going," Paddy announced, nudging Marcel. The two birds took flight.

"What are you doing here?" Kate asked Humphrey as he approached.

He reached back into his fur and pulled out a flower. "A little something for your big day," he told her, sliding it gently into her fur. She gazed into his eyes, so close their noses were almost touching. Her heart ached.

Then he stepped back. "I just wanted to say good-bye."

"Good-bye?"

"Yeah. I'm thinking about doing some traveling," Humphrey continued. "Seeing where the train takes me. Maybe I'll visit our friends the bears—our old buddies. See how they're doing." He managed a weak smile. "I'll tell 'em you said hi."

Kate was still processing what he'd said. "Wait, you're leaving Jasper?"

"Yeah, you know—it's a lone wolf thing."

"Well, I know Humphrey the fun-loving Omega," Kate tried to joke, "but not Humphrey the lone wolf."

"So I'll be a fun-loving lone wolf." That got a brief smile from her, and Humphrey echoed it. Then he turned and loped off. Kate watched him go until he'd vanished into the trees. Then she forced herself to swivel back toward the valley below. But one paw rose to touch the flower in her fur, stroking it gently.

# CHAPTER NINE

The sun was shining bright and clear in a perfect blue sky when Kate met Garth on a large, flat boulder in the center of the valley. Wolves from both packs were gathered all around them.

"So," Garth asked her quietly, "are you ready?"

Kate nodded. She had to be.

"Good." He didn't meet her eyes when he said it, though, and he seemed skittish.

"Are you okay?" she asked him softly.

"Ha ha, you bet," he answered. "No problems on this end. Ready to go, go, go!" He puffed up his chest and raised his head proudly, but Kate didn't miss the way his eyes flickered to the side. Curious, she glanced over that way, only to see Lilly there, a sad little frown still on her face. What was that all about?

"So, you wanna start this thing or should I?" Garth asked her.

"We'll start together," Kate decided. That was the whole point, after all. Uniting the packs. Nothing was more important than that. Nothing.

"Start together. Yeah." Garth took a deep breath, and he and Kate both stepped closer, then slid past each other slightly so that their muzzles were close to each other's flanks. They leaned in closer, each sniffing at the other to show they were accepting their new mate's scent, and Kate closed her eyes. In her mind she pictured a different wolf beside her: with an infectious smile.

Humphrey was racing along through the park. Up ahead he could just spot the telltale plume of smoke whizzing through the trees. It was the train.

A fluttering sound descended upon him, and he glanced up but didn't slow down as Marcel and Paddy appeared, flying alongside.

"Do you think I can make it?" he asked them, panting from the effort.

"Yes, sir," Paddy replied. "I see the train coming. And just as you hit the tracks you should see an open train car."

"Good luck," Marcel added.

Humphrey laughed. "Thanks, guys."

He put on an extra burst of speed and pulled ahead of them. Now he could see the long, sleek shape of the train hurtling along. There was nothing here in Jasper Park for him anymore. It was time to move on.

Kate and Garth had progressed from sniffing each other's scents to nuzzling each other's ears. Now they both backed away a pace or two, until they were looking into each other's eyes. There was only one step left—rubbing noses. Once they did that, they would be mates for life. The packs would be united, and so would they. Forever.

Kate looked at Garth. She could see from his grimace and his sad eyes that he wasn't in love with her, either. Was this really right? To spend the rest of her life with someone who she didn't love and who didn't love her? Their marriage would unite the packs, but could anything really survive and flourish if it was built on something so hollow?

Garth had closed his eyes and raised his nose, feeling for her. She couldn't do this!

"Kate?" Garth whispered under his breath. "What are you doing?" He was clearly waiting for her.

But now that Kate had made her decision, she knew it felt right. She backed away from Garth and glanced around. But how was she going to explain this?

"Kate?" Garth had opened his eyes now, and was watching her.

"I can't," she told him.

He started to laugh, and Kate saw real relief wash across his face. "You can't!" Then he remembered where they were and put on a hangdog expression. "I mean—you can't?"

"What is this?" Tony demanded, prowling forward until his front paws rested on the lip of the boulder. "Winston? Why can't she marry Garth?"

"Quiet!" Winston roared. He approached from his side. "Kate," he said softly, leaning in so his head was almost touching hers. "Why can't you marry Garth?"

Kate shook her head. She hated to disappoint her father and let down the pack. But she had to follow her heart.

"Because," she told him, lifting her head and raising her voice so everyone could hear her, "I fell in love with an Omega!"

A gasp rippled through the assembled wolves.

"An Omega?" Winston staggered back. Beside him, Eve actually fainted, collapsing on the valley floor. Some of the Omegas—particularly Humphrey's buddies—were grinning, though. And Kate thought she saw a small smile cross Lilly's lips.

Humphrey had reached the clearing, and the train snaked along in front of him. Up ahead he spotted a small mound, perfect for making the leap onto the train. And there was the open boxcar door Paddy had mentioned. Perfect.

He concentrated, judging speed, distance, and angle, when another thought washed all that away. The memory of his last train ride overwhelmed him, and especially howling with Kate as the moon shone overhead.

But that had been last night. Everything had changed now. Humphrey shook his head to drive all that away, and focused once more. He was reaching the mound now. He crouched as he ran, flexing and coiling his legs, and then, just as he hit the mound's peak, he leaped! His future awaited!

Winston was still confused, but Tony was furious. "An Omega?" he growled. "Ha ha ha! An Alpha in love with an Omega! That's against pack law!"

"Dad!" Garth's shout took everyone by surprise, and all eyes turned toward him. But this time Garth didn't seem nervous at all as he raised his head proudly and declared, "I'm also in love with an Omega!" He leaped off the boulder—and loped straight to Lilly! She beamed at him and moved forward to touch her nose to his.

Kate was amazed. Garth—and her little sister? No wonder Lilly had been upset when helping her get ready! *Go, little sister,* Kate cheered silently. *You deserve it!* She could tell, too, that Garth adored Lilly, and revised her opinion of him. Anyone who loved Lilly that much couldn't be all that bad.

Of course, Garth's father was less than pleased with this turn of events. "What have you done to my son, Winston?" Tony demanded. He paced toward Winston, who was still shaking his head.

"An Alpha and an Omega?" Kate heard her father muttering. "An Alpha and an Omega."

"This isn't our custom!" Tony insisted. "This isn't our way!" He had worked himself into a fervor, and spun to face his pack. "Take the valley!" he shouted.

The eastern pack wolves howled out a war cry when they heard his order, and charged forward. It only took the western pack Alphas a heartbeat to respond with howls and leaps of their own. Kate's blood chilled as she saw the packs racing toward each other, intent once more upon war.

Then she saw something beyond the other wolves.

A dust cloud was billowing up from the valley's far end, and it was rapidly flowing toward them. A rushing sound traveled with it, and then it rounded a corner and Kate could make out a mass of large, dark shapes within it. The caribou! They had probably been skittish already, smelling so many wolves nearby, and now with all the growling and howling they had finally panicked. She quickly found her voice and raised her head, hoping her cry would carry over the sounds of impending battle.

"Stampede!" she bellowed as loud as she could. "Stampede!"

# CHAPTER TEN

The horde of snarling wolves stopped in their tracks. Tony and Winston took charge immediately. "Everyone—run!" Winston shouted. "Run!"

"To the sides of the valley!" Tony added. The battle was forgotten as every wolf scattered toward the valley walls. Kate was swept along in the tide of fur and paws, and finally managed to pull free only after she had reached relative safety.

Winston and Tony still stood in the center of the valley. As pack leaders, they had a responsibility to make sure their packs reached safety. Finally the two Alphas deemed their wolves far enough out of harm's way, and turned to run themselves. But no sooner had they taken a dozen strides then Tony faltered to a stop and screamed in pain.

"*Agh!*" he cried out. "It's that darn disc in my back!" He began writhing about.

Winston circled back and thwacked Tony hard on the back with one paw. It seemed to help and a second later he was able to move again. He was shaky, though, and no faster than a cub.

Winston never left his side. They had been friends and allies long before they'd been adversaries.

But Kate could see the caribou sweeping toward them. "Oh, no!" she whispered. "They're trapped!"

Winston snapped at the first few caribou to come close, and they swerved to avoid his sharp teeth. The caribou behind them followed their lead, but it was only a matter of time before that gap closed, and now both sides were cut off. There was only one direction Winston and Tony could go: farther down the valley.

Kate knew what she had to do. There was only one chance to save them — she would have to somehow get to the two elder wolves and pull them out of the caribou's path. She started running, heading down a ridge that ran along the side of the valley, picking up speed as she went. She drew even with the first caribou, then passed them. A little farther and she'd be able to turn around and leap down into their midst. It was dangerous for her, but it was the only way to save Tony and her father.

The other wolves were all keeping to the valley walls, staying well clear of the stampede, so Kate was surprised when she saw a gray blur racing toward her. Humphrey! He'd come back!

"Humphrey!" she called as they neared each other. "Humphrey!"

"Kate!" He skidded to a stop beside her, panting hard, and she stopped as well.

"You came back!" she whispered.

"I couldn't leave," he admitted just as softly. "Everything I really want is here."

Kate couldn't forget her mission, however—she allowed herself only a second of bliss before looking away. "We have to help them," she explained, gesturing down toward the valley.

Humphrey nodded. He'd seen the stampede as he'd arrived, and had been racing to look for Kate and make sure she was okay. But he understood. She couldn't let her father die.

But Kate shook her head. "I don't know what to do," she admitted. "There's nowhere they'd be safe."

Then Humphrey spotted something else, something not in the valley but above it. "Look!" He pointed, and Kate turned. An old log was sitting below them on the ridge, angled down into the valley.

"Are you thinking what I'm thinking?" Humphrey asked her.

"Yeah," Kate responded, bounding past him. "Where are those bears when we need them?"

They hopped onto the log together, and leaned forward. Their combined weight tilted it down, and it pulled free of the moss and grass and ivy that had held it there. It began to slide down the slope.

"Roll left!" Humphrey shouted. He'd taken the lead, and Kate didn't argue. She shifted to the left, and the log angled with them, slipping past a tree. "Roll left again!" They angled past another tree.

Humphrey was panting, and so Kate saw the next obstacle before he did. "Roll left again!" she ordered, and this time it was Humphrey who obeyed without question.

Then she glanced down toward the valley floor. "Oh, no!" She moaned, gauging the distance to Winston and Tony. "We'll never make it. They're too far ahead!"

Humphrey scanned the area, looking for something to give them an edge—and found it. "Hold on!" he warned, and threw his weight to the right. The log angled sharply and sailed toward a cliff jutting out over the valley. They hit it with a jarring impact and gripped tight with their claws as the log flew out into the air.

Winston and Tony were still running but neither one was a young wolf anymore, and they were faltering. The caribou were closing in around them. Suddenly—

*Crash!* A log slammed to the ground right in front

of them. Two wolves went tumbling off it, landing on its far side. With a start Winston realized it was Kate—and Humphrey!

"Come on!" Kate urged. Winston wasted no time leaping over the log and huddling behind it next to his daughter. Tony followed quickly. And just in time! They were safe!

Humphrey smiled at Kate. "World adventurers," he reminded her.

She laughed. "I told you we'd make a good team."

He acted surprised. "Did you say that? I thought I said that."

She lifted her head to make a retort—and collided with the legs of a caribou that was just clearing the log. *Smack!* Kate's eyes fluttered, her jaw went slack, and she collapsed, rolling away from the log.

"Kate!" Humphrey was up in an instant. He leaped forward and covered her body with his own. *Wham!* A caribou hoof pounded him in the back. *Whack!* Another caught him in the head. But he gritted his teeth and refused to move.

Winston and Tony had seen the whole thing, and

they were right behind Humphrey. They turned and snarled, howling and lunging at the caribou racing toward them, their energy restored. The pack leaders' ferocity cowed the caribou, which swerved around them again, leaving the stricken couple untouched. But were they too late?

# CHAPTER ELEVEN

After what seemed like an eternity the last of the herd had passed them by, and were now thundering down the valley. Humphrey pulled himself off of Kate, wincing at each bruise and scrape. But he forgot his own aches and pains as he gazed down upon her.

"Kate!" he whispered. "Kate!"

He nudged her gently with the tip of his nose. She didn't move.

Winston and Tony came to stand beside him, and slowly the rest of both packs gathered around them as well.

"Please, Kate," Humphrey pleaded, nuzzling the back of her neck. "Please. You can't do this."

Still nothing.

Finally he rested his head on her shoulder. Tears were dripping down his face and falling onto her fur, soaking into her skin, as Humphrey shifted until his mouth was right beside her ear.

"I love you," he told her softly. He wished he'd said it back on the train. Now she would never hear him.

The sadness swelled within him until he threw his head back and howled his pain to the world.

Beside him, Winston stepped closer until they were shoulder to shoulder. Then he lifted his own majestic head and added his voice to Humphrey's, expressing his grief at the loss of his beloved daughter.

Lilly and Eve joined in, and then all of the western pack wolves, sharing their sorrow.

Then another voice, young, strong, and earnest, joined its notes to theirs. Garth! The eastern pack wolf howled with them, and soon others from his pack were sharing in the howl. Even Tony finally could not resist. They were pack animals, and both packs were united in this moment of intense loss.

The sound of howling filled the air—so many wolves, but a single cause and a single voice. All of them poured themselves into their cries, muzzles raised up to the sky—

—and so it was that at first none of them noticed movement on the ground by Humphrey's feet.

"*Uhh . . .*" Kate groaned and turned her head, then gasped as the world threatened to tilt sideways on her. What had happened? And what was all the howling? It felt like a hundred wolves, all crying at once, had surrounded her!

She stirred and blinked, then blinked again. Finally she lifted her head, trying to make sense of what she was seeing. Both packs . . . together? Howling?

Her feeble motions finally broke through Humphrey's daze, and his howling cut off abruptly. "Kate?" He leaned in to nuzzle her. "Kate!"

"Humphrey?" Kate sat up, then swayed and almost fell. Humphrey pressed his shoulder against her side to steady her.

"I thought I lost you," he told her gently.

The howling around them was dying down in

waves. Soon the cries had been replaced by laughter and conversation, but still there was no fighting. Howling together had buried any enmity that might have existed between the two packs.

"Is everyone staring at us?" Kate asked Humphrey after a minute. She forced herself to her feet and took a deep breath. The pain was starting to fade.

"Well, uh, no," Humphrey assured her. He glanced around. "Not every . . . well, yeah, now they are."

Kate decided she didn't care. "Aw, darn," she said, putting on a pout. "'Cause I wanted to tell you something." She leaned in close and whispered in his ear, the words she'd been feeling for some time but hadn't dared say.

Humphrey acted surprised. "What? Really?" He laughed, and Kate couldn't help but smile. "Okay. Well." He took a deep breath of his own. "I wanted to tell you something, too. I love you."

Kate giggled and nuzzled him, and he nuzzled her in return. Everything was going to be fine.

"Maybe this can work," Kate heard her father say quietly. He was still standing beside them.

"Oh, I—" Tony started to protest, but a fierce growl cut him off as Eve leaned in toward him, her teeth bared. "All right!" Tony yelped quickly. Then he sighed. "All right."

On their other side Kate heard a happy yelp. She looked up in time to see Lilly leap toward Garth and tackle him, sending the two of them tumbling on the grass. Kate chuckled.

All around them, wolves began to pick up on their joy, and began to dance and howl. Soon the entire valley was filled with happy, cavorting wolves. And why not? The packs were united at last. There would be no more fighting over food, no more squabbling over territory. They were all one big pack now. And—Kate turned and touched noses with Humphrey—they were in love!

She lifted her muzzle to the sky and began to howl from pure joy. Humphrey joined her, and their twined voices washed across the other wolves and over the valley itself. They were an Alpha and an Omega in love, and nothing could be better.

The hilarious movie *Alpha and Omega* stars wildly different wolf friends Humphrey and Kate of the western pack.

Of course, wolves in real life are a little different than the ones in *Alpha and Omega*. Wolves are nearly extinct in many areas, and their lives in the wild are even more difficult and uncertain than the lives of wolves in the packs of *Alpha and Omega*. Wolves spend their time hunting throughout their territories, working hard to find enough food to feed their packs. They are highly intelligent, loyal, and loving to their families and fierce in their protection of them.

Wolves are wild predators and have many unique characteristics that make them ideally suited to live and thrive in the wilderness. Wolves have broad heads; narrow chests; long, strong legs; and large paws. They are built for speed and agility over all types of terrain, including deep snow. Wolves usually trot along at about five miles per hour. They easily roam about twelve miles a day. At top speed, wolves can run as fast as forty miles per hour for short distances. The distance between their tracks can be as far as six to eight feet! The way that wolves step helps them cover long distances efficiently, as the hind paws falls into the same impression the front paws left. This really helps them in snow or on difficult terrain. Wolves are also excellent swimmers because their toes have webbing between them.

As seen in *Alpha and Omega*, not all wolves look alike. Most wolves are shades of golden or reddish brown with hints of black, white, gold, cream, or darker brown fur. This blend of color gives the wolf its "gray" camouflage coloring and helps it blend into the shadows from spring through fall. Wolves have two layers of fur. The outer or "guard" layer consists of long, coarse hairs which shed water and snow. These are the hairs that give each coat its individual color. The short, thick undercoat is a layer of soft, light-colored fur. This is called a "prime coat." It traps air and insulates the wolf from the elements.

In the wintertime, wolves' coats grow very thick. These layers are so warm that wolves are comfortable in temperatures far below zero. They wrap their thick bushy tail across their faces and sleep curled up under the snow! In spring, they shed their undercoat to stay cool during the hotter summer weather.

In general, from their nose to the tip of their tail, wolves can be five to eight feet long! An adult male wolf usually weighs seventy-five to one hundred and twenty pounds, and adult females weigh between sixty and ninety-five pounds. Northern gray wolves are the largest wolf species and are larger and heavier than wolves which live in hotter climates. A wolf lives only eight to ten years in the wild, but can live up to eighteen years in captivity.

Wolves' eye color is blue at birth, changing to green, brown, gray, or yellowish gold at about eight weeks of age. Wolves have excellent night and side vision and are very good at detecting motion.

## The Nose Knows

A wolf's keen sense of smell is its most highly

developed sense. It is also its most important asset. Researchers believe that wolves' sense of smell is one hundred times better than a human's and even twenty five times better than an average dog's. Wolves use their sense of smell to locate prey and track them through difficult terrain. Wolves can detect the smell of other animals up to one and three quarters of a mile away.

Scents play an important role in communication between wolves. Wolves signal the boundaries of their territory by "marking" the areas with their particular smell. They paw and kick around these markings to spread more odors from the scent glands they have between their toes. As they travel around their territory, wolves can smell these markings and tell who left them there, when, and probably their age and gender. In this way, they keep track of the movements of their own pack and of other wolves in the area. Wolves also have scent glands under and on top of the tail, and on their face. When one wolf greets another, they smell all these areas to learn about the other wolf's identity, health, and mood.

## Diet

Even working together, it is hard for wolves to catch their prey. As the pack learned in *Alpha and Omega*, caribou are hard for wolves to catch and an entire herd can be very dangerous! Wolves must be careful: Sharp hooves can easily injure or even kill them. Luckily, Kate had Humphrey to protect her during the stampede in Jasper Park! The animals that wolves catch are usually old, sick, or very young, and can be separated more easily from the rest of the herd. Wolves will also eat rabbits, rats, mice, birds, snakes, fish, and other small animals. They will even occasionally eat earthworms, berries, and grasshoppers.

When they find food or make a kill, wolves eat as much as they can. A single wolf can eat twenty pounds of meat at one time. Wolves eat their food very quickly to protect it from being stolen. Plus they wouldn't want to be eating if another predator or wolf pack showed up. They eat the best parts first, and come back later for the remainder. They will hide food in the snow or icy soil, which helps to preserve it and protect it from scavengers. Wolves can eat every six hours when they have plenty of food. But, when there is little food to be found, they can live on scraps for up to two weeks at a time.

## Young Wolves

Wolf pups, or cubs, are born from April to late May, depending on the climate. Pups are born earlier in warmer areas and later in colder spots. They stay with their mothers in a cozy den for the first three weeks of their lives. The den can be a cave, a hollow log, or a hole the mother digs in the ground. A litter averages five or six pups. The new wolf pups are born blind and deaf. They can't maintain their body heat at first and would die without the protection of their mother's body. The mother stays in the den for the first four weeks, except for quick trips out for water. All the pups do is eat and sleep!

Both parents share the responsibility of caring for the cubs. The mother's mate and the other pack members guard the den, hunt, and bring the mother back all the food she needs. After three weeks the pups' eyes open. After about four weeks they begin to hear and their first teeth break through their gums so they can start to eat solid food. When the mother finally begins to leave the den to hunt for food, the pups come, too.

The adults bring meat back to the pups at the den, sometimes carrying it many miles. The easiest way they can do this is to carry it in their stomachs! The pups lick the muzzles of the adults when they return from hunting, which helps the adults cough up the extra food. The growing pups eagerly eat all the meat they can get to help them grow.

The other adult pack members are usually the pups' older brothers and sisters. They look after the pups as though they were their own. One adult is always with the pups or very nearby, guarding them.

The pups are strong for their size and grow and mature very quickly. When they are born, they each weigh about a pound. After about two months, the pups begin to look more like the adults. Their ears, muzzles, and bodies lengthen and stretch out and the pups weigh fifteen to twenty pounds.

When the pups are about six weeks old, they

begin to follow after the adults as they set off on a hunt. But they tend to give up when they are tired and return to the den to wait. As they get older and stronger, they are able to follow the adults to the hunt, even though they are still too young to join in. At this time, the whole pack abandons the den where the cubs were born and moves to a new temporary den called a "rendezvous site." Here, the young cubs have a small rough den hidden in a thicket or dug out under some rocks just large enough for them to sleep and hide, if necessary. This new site is much closer to the current area where the wolves are hunting, and could be as far as twenty miles away from where the pups were born.

Wolf pups love to play. They use bones or bits of animal skin as toys. They attack their "toys" and carry them around proudly. They also stalk and pounce on their siblings and older pack members—just like Kate and Lilly did in *Alpha and Omega*. This is good practice, and, as soon as they can, they begin to hunt small animals like mice. When the pups are old enough, the pack starts to bring the pups to the kills rather than carrying pieces of meat back to them. When all growing juvenile wolves can keep up with the pack as they hunt, the pack abandons the rendezvous site altogether. Except for the time when the pups are in their den, wolves travel throughout their territory. They may seek shelter to rest, but they prefer to spend their time in the open, searching for their prey. The young adults usually stay in their pack for two to three years until they reach their full growth and maturity. This gives them time to learn the skills of survival and get plenty of experience before they set out on their own.

Young adult wolves eventually leave their family and go looking for a mate and a territory where they can form a new pack. This is known as "dispersing." In the wild, Humphrey and Kate probably would have left and gone back to the Sawtooth National Forest in Idaho to start their own pack once they were married. It was a perfect place for a new wolf pair! Young wolves scatter in different directions, looking for an area free of other wolf pack scent markers and also looking for another lone wolf of the opposite sex. This is a difficult task. In any wolf population, at a given time, some five to twenty percent of wolves are lone wolves. Many dispersing wolves are unsuccessful at finding a mate and territory for themselves. A wolf's original pack will often welcome the young adult back into the pack if that happens. There they can wait until conditions improve, and they can try again to form their own family.

In the wild, if two lone wolves meet while out on their own, and are attracted to each other, they will court and attempt to form a pair bond. If successful, they will travel about together, trying to set up a territory for their future pack. The new pack may be established close to the birth pack, or the new pack may be formed hundreds of miles away. This helps wolves spread into distant new areas. Wolves develop strong emotional bonds, and usually mate for life.

## Wolf Packs

Wolves are highly developed social animals. Wolves live, travel, and hunt in packs that include the mother and father wolves, their pups, and several other lower ranking adults—usually their grown children. In many ways a wolf pack is like a human family. It is the parent wolves who exercise authority. Because they dominate the behaviors of the other wolves in the pack, they are often referred to as the Alpha male and the Alpha female and are the pack leaders. They direct the tracking and hunting of prey, choose the den location, and establish the pack's territory. Wolves often demonstrate deep affection for their family and may even sacrifice themselves to protect the family unit.

Average pack size is from five to eight wolves, but can swell to between twenty and thirty if two or three litters of cubs are born in one year. The largest known wolf packs are found in Canada and Alaska. Sometimes, in a large pack that has plentiful food, one or more of the packs' grown children may bring in an outside mate, and the pack may have two litters in a single year.

Wolf packs may split up if the pack becomes too large for all the wolves to get along well, or if there isn't enough food. If this happens and the territory is large enough, the two packs may simply split the old territory. Or a pack may split up if both of the Alpha wolves die. If only one of the Alpha wolves die, the remaining Alpha wolf usually takes a new mate, and continues their pack leadership.

Wolves living in packs have the advantage over lone wolves. There are more adults to help with the hunt, spreading out around the game, and increasing the rate of success. Mother wolves can give birth and nurse their pups with more success when both her mate and the other adults can bring her food. A pack with several adults can better defend its territory against other wolves who may try to invade and take over their territory.

## Communication

Wolves communicate often with their family and members of their pack. The most well-known way they do this is through their spine-tingling howls. It is considered a very special experience to get to hear the actual live howls of these endangered animals.

Although many stories and pictures portray wolves howling at a full moon, wolves do not howl at the moon. Howls are used in different ways for communication. A full moon seems to have little effect on wolves, other than to provide them with more light at night for hunting. They howl anytime, day or night, but more often at dawn and dusk, when they are most active. The howl of a wolf can be heard up to ten miles away, especially by other wolves, which have very keen hearing.

A lone wolf will howl to locate a mate, or to relocate their pack if they have been separated. The pack will scatter out when hunting and use howls to keep track of each other as they run. If a wolf finds a likely prey animal, it will call the others with a special howl. Wolves also howl more often while raising their pups, probably teaching them what they need to know about pack communication. A chorus howl is three or more wolves howling together. Studies show that there are many reasons why several wolves howl together. They howl as a way to unite the pack, before a hunt, or to celebrate their successful return from a hunt. Sometimes the whole pack comes together for a social "rally," howling and wagging their tails and sniffing noses. Wolves also respond as a chorus to the howls of a rival pack, warning them away from their territory. Chorus howls move up and down, using high and low notes, stopping and starting again, making it very difficult for a rival pack to tell how many wolves are howling. It is smart for a small pack to sound larger than it actually is! In a duet, two wolves howl together, either taking turns or howling at the same time.

Of course, howling is just one of the many ways that wolves communicate. They bark, yip, pant, squeak, whine, and growl. They also communicate through facial expressions, gestures, body postures, and tail postures. Wolves bark to warn other pack members of danger or to challenge an enemy, such as a bear or coyote. They often growl at each other in dominance disputes or other kinds of threatening encounters.

## Social Stats

Researchers can't be absolutely certain what the different sounds, postures, and expressions really mean, but biologists have been able to draw pretty good conclusions about the ways that wolves communicate with each other. Early studies of adult wolves in captivity resulted in the designations of Alpha, Beta, and Omega wolf rankings. These designations have not been found to be very true in more current studies of wolves in the wild. Most wild wolf packs are small, between five and eight members and are the extended family of a mated Alpha wolf pair, including some of their adult offspring. Only rarely is an unrelated adult even allowed to join. In the wild, most challenges and fights occur between wolves of neighboring packs as they fight for territory and hunting rights, or to drive off a lone wolf looking for a new territory. The movie *Alpha and Omega* simply divides wolves into two ranks: dominant Alphas and peacekeeping Omegas. But it's more complicated in real packs in the wild.

Researchers have found that the mated Alpha

male and female wolves are the highest ranking wolves. They lead the pack. The Alpha wolves are usually the only pair in the pack to have pups. The Alpha male is in charge of the males and the Alpha female is in charge of the females. The Alpha pair also decides when and where to hunt, when to rest, and where the pack makes their den. Also, the Alpha pair and their offspring from the current year eat first at a kill.

The rank or social order of the pack determines the actions and behaviors of each individual wolf. Which wolves hold the higher rank, and how their rank is enforced, can be quite different between packs and between individual animals. Personality and attitude are more important than size or physical strength in deciding which wolf will be the highest ranking. Dominant wolves generally act more confident than submissive ones. Older sisters and brothers usually hold a higher rank than the younger pack members. Rank changes in a pack as young pups mature and as young adults leave to find a mate and form packs of their own.

Wolves spend most of their time acting in a neutral way around the other wolves in their pack. If needed, they change their expressions toward dominance or submission depending on which other wolves they interact with. An Alpha wolf will often simply glare hard at a wolf to send it a dominance message, and a submissive wolf will often just look away to give the right response. At greetings or other interactions, a wolf showing dominance will stand tall, look the other wolf in the eyes, point the ears forward, and lift the tail slightly up. Younger Alpha wolves showing submission will look away from the other wolf, put their ears back, scrunch slightly down, and tuck their tails. These subtle displays reassure the pack that all is well.

If a wolf's position and rank is really threatened, the higher ranking wolf may growl or snarl, wrinkle its forehead, show its teeth, bump or slam into the other wolf, or even hold it down. When the submissive wolf gives in, its stronger signals include tucking their tail, whining and pawing at the dominant wolf, even rolling over and exposing the throat and whimpering. Sometimes a challenge for rank results in a fight, and the losing wolf could be driven out of the pack. Such fighting does not occur often. Wolves need each other and cannot spend all their time and energy fighting!

## Behavior

Playing and having fun is important to wolves. Like their cousin, the dog, they will bow down with their hindquarters up and tail wagging to invite their pack members to play. Through play, pups learn the skills they need for hunting and communication. The more they play, the stronger they become, and the earliest rank is determined through play. Adult wolves also love to play. They really seem to enjoy wrestling, chasing each other, and playing tag.

## Hunting

Hunting wolves work as a team. Males and females hunt together. Making use of the element of surprise, wolves quietly sneak up on a weak or older animal at the edge of a herd, or lie in wait until it comes near.

They follow the lead of the Alpha wolves who are usually the first to start the chase and actually attack the prey. Wolves prefer their prey to run so they can injure a leg, bringing the animal down so it's easier to go in for the kill.

It's all part of the cycle of nature. By hunting weak, sick, or older animals from a herd, there is more food available to the young and healthy animals—which is good for the caribou and elk. Wolves are very wary of humans, and attacks on humans are extremely rare and almost always involve a wolf that is rabid or sick. But all large predators like wolves are potentially dangerous and should be avoided by humans.

## Wolves in History

Wolves have survived since the Ice Ages, for over 300,000 years, and once lived freely throughout the world's northern hemisphere. Hundreds of years ago, there were probably as many as two million wolves living throughout the world. Now it is estimated that there are only about 200,000 wolves worldwide, despite the recent efforts by many countries to re-populate them.

Wolves were not always feared. Native tribes in Canada and America respected and revered the wolf, considering them "brothers" and spirit guides. These tribes adapted their likenesses as totem animals, and used wolf furs and teeth in ceremonies and for jewelry. Legends were told of the intelligent hunting behavior of the wolf pack and also of the love and dedication the wolf showed its family. But even in these areas, wolves were trapped mercilessly out of fear, to protect livestock, or for their fur. As a result, many wolves were hunted nearly to extinction.

The wolves that survived did so by retreating into even wilder, less populated areas. In Russia, where there are large areas of wilderness, the largest wolf population in the world has survived. The world's second largest wolf population is found in the remote wilderness areas of Canada and Alaska. A few small wolf populations also survived in isolated areas of eastern Europe, China, and India. Wolves are now extinct in England, western European nations, and in the lower forty-eight states of America and Mexico.

After wolves became extinct in the lower United States and Europe, biologists began to realize that these great predators had long held a very important place in the natural order of our ecosystems. Studies have shown that the lack of large predators such as the wolf allowed elk and deer to overpopulate. This, in turn, led to overgrazing of trees and other important plants. That meant less food for other animals like beavers and birds. Wolves also help keep mice, rats, and rabbits under control so that these small animals don't destroy the plants needed by yet other wildlife species for both food and shelter. Keeping our ecosystems balanced with as many naturally occurring animals and plants as possible make our world a healthier, more diverse, and beautiful place to live.

## Species

There are several different species of wolves still living in the wilderness. The gray wolf is the largest. It is found in Canada, Alaska, and the northern parts of the United States. Some other subspecies of the gray wolf are found in specific areas of North America and Eurasia. Arctic wolves, tundra wolves, Iberian wolves, eastern timber wolves, Italian wolves, Russian Wolves, Mexican wolves, great plains wolves, northwestern wolves, and arabian wolves are all gray wolves.

The red wolf can be found in the wild in one area of North Carolina in the southeastern United States, and is still considered especially threatened. Some of the other wolf species found throughout Europe, Asia, Russia, and China are the Eurasian wolf, the Indian wolf, and the Ethiopian wolf.

In Canada today, it is estimated that there is a gray, arctic, and timber wolf population of between 52,000 and 60,000 wolves. In Alaska, there are between 8,000 and 11,000 gray and arctic wolves. Just as Kate and Humphrey in *Alpha and Omega* were captured in Jasper Park and taken to the Sawtooth National Forest, some of these gray wolf pairs were actually relocated from Canada to the United States in 1995. Wolves are slowly dispersing naturally to Washington, Oregon, Utah, Colorado, North Dakota, and South Dakota with a few sightings in each state. North Carolina is home to about 100 red wolves recently introduced back into the wild. Finally, Mexican wolves or *lobos* have been reintroduced to parks in Arizona and New Mexico, with less than ninety wolves living there.

## Wolves in Danger

In the United States and Canada, the numbers of wolves are being managed, with some hunting allowed as populations rise and they get too close to ranches or farms. Experts are working with livestock owners to develop methods to reduce the numbers of wolves killed for attacking livestock. These methods include fencing livestock, lighting, alarm systems, and removing dead or dying livestock that may attract wolves.

In the United States, since 1974, most wolves have been protected under the Endangered Species Act as an endangered or threatened species. The Endangered Species Act requires the federal government to identify species threatened with extinction, identify habitats they need to survive, and help protect both. Many other countries throughout the world are working to put similar protection in place for threatened wildlife in their ecosystems.

In *Alpha and Omega*, the eastern and western packs resolve their differences and unite their packs. There is enough food for everyone, and the caribou, bears, squirrels, geese, and ducks all live happily ever after in their beautiful wilderness home. As people around the globe continue to value our natural and biological heritage and support wildlife and ecological efforts, wolves will continue to multiply and prosper in our natural wilderness areas, helping to restore the natural balance.

# Follow all the adventures with Alpha and Omega books!

Available wherever books are sold!

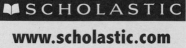

**SCHOLASTIC**

**www.scholastic.com**

A&01